Dancing on
Barbed Wire

What Writers and Editors Are Saying about
Dancing on Barbed Wire

The voices of Terry Dalrymple, Jerry Craven and Andrew Geyer blend within and across these excellent stories to produce the satisfying effect of a finely crafted novel. In "Sandjack Carson and the Schoolmarm," the opening story, Paul Gruffyn Beaty, the narrator, promises what the book delivers, "though the telling be difficult and fraught with guilt and blood." There is guilt and blood aplenty. But what follows is more, a tapestry of legend and lore, myth and romance in this chronicle of love and loss, family and friendship, failure and redemption. Here characters from the pioneer past and the chaotic present are haunted by an ancient, elusive code and surrounded by the beauty and brutality that is the eternal landscape of rural Texas. Dancing on Barbed Wire is an innovative saga, a marvelous achievement.
—Phillip Gardner, author of *Available Light*

With jaggedly barbed wit, these stories of likable, flawed folks from small-town Texas will make you laugh out loud—until they make you cry—when they pivot on the lyrical magic of language and the fathomless weavings of destiny in the characters' lives. Along the way you'll discover that you, like these characters, have been dancing on barbed wire.
—Lynn Hoggard, author of *Motherland: Stories and Poems of Louisiana*

These tales could take place in Maine or Alaska, Minnesota or Alabama. They're about human beings doing the best they can to figure things out. Messrs Dalrymple, Craven, and Geyer have a finger on the pulse, a stethoscope to the heart, in *Dancing on Barbed Wire*, whether it be traditional-length story, flash fiction, or novella.
—George Singleton, author of *Calloustown* and 6 other story collections

These narratives, written by Texas' three of Texas' finest living fiction writers, crisscross the state, revealing its rugged charm. The characters you'll meet in this book are some real pieces of work—from bastards to drunks to feral cat wranglers—but in each of them, we find flashes of redemption, beauty, and grace. Craven, Dalrymple and Geyer show the power of artistic collaboration and challenge the notion of the solitary writer. The result is a multifaceted, engaging, and real collection of short fiction that captures the complexity of contemporary life in Texas. *Dancing on Barbed Wire* is a triumph!

—Katie Hoerth, Editor-in-chief, Lamar University Literary Press and author of *The Lost Chronicles of Slue Foot Sue*

Co-authors Terry Dalrymple, Jerry Craven and Andrew Geyer deliver the excitement promised in the title and then some as they propel the reader through 171 pages of love, lust, betrayal and redemption. The sixteen interlocked narratives move at a clip through time and space, from the Civil War to the present, from sun-scorched brush country to the lush and sometimes lethal Piney Woods. Although readers may detect shades of Hawthorne and Faulkner in the haunted houses, serial characters, disembodied voices and rattling family skeletons appearing in these stories, their ethos is distinctly Texan, complete with fields of swaying bluebonnets, sprawling ranches, a champion roping horse and plenty of three-alarm chile. The authors deftly sidestep stereotypes, however, instead showcasing such unexpected characters as a cowboy who hates cattle, a parrot that curses mailmen, and a Hill Country farmer who prays to the Roman goddess Fortuna. Reading this story cycle is like doing a jigsaw puzzle--there's no mistaking the satisfaction of snapping that final piece into place and admiring the master narrative that suddenly emerges. Bravo!

—Carol Coffee Reposa, 2018 Texas Poet Laureate and author of *Underground Musicians*

Dalrymple, Craven, and Geyer conspire wonderfully to illustrate the many faces of story telling. Though complex in form, the core of this collection is an illustration in itself of excellence in the craft of fiction. The book's central theme is love, loss, and lust, and these authors "dancing on barb wire" never slip, never fall, and they always entertain. They convince and make the reader believe, the crucial test of art. The myriad ways in which a story can be told is their subject, and like all things human the way of telling is the way of truth.

—Gerald Duff, author of *Nashville Burning*, *Playing Custer*, and other novels

This clever adaptation of the short-story cycle is like a weaving where characters pass first as warp—setting the stage, then weft—elaborating their histories and motives. The reader meets again a character from a previous story, with more revelation through widening circumstances. Texas folk, mostly rural or small-town, of Southeast and Southwest Texas stomp and holler, suffer, try to explain themselves to others, to find in the end they only need to explain themselves to themselves. It's an added bonus that the three authors are longtime friends, acting through an art form as though they were standing together under a mesquite tree, drinking beer, finishing each other's sentences.

—Jan Seale, Texas Poet Laureate, 2012, author of *Ordinary Charms*

For over two decades, I have followed, with keen interest and deep respect, the distinguished fiction of Jerry Craven, Terry Dalrymple, and Andrew Geyer. In *Dancing on Barbed Wire*, the three authors join their considerable talents to create a cutting-edge "anthology" of twelve short stories, three pieces of flash fiction, and a novella, all of which are intricately linked by character, plot, setting (Texas), theme, imagery, and style. None of the authors is identified in the text of the book. The three authors merge their individual voices so seamlessly into a single "new voice" that it is impossible for me to identify "who" writes "what," despite my longtime familiarity with the fiction of all three. The deft manipulation of literary voice which characterizes this breakthrough work of fiction is stunningly original and executed with consummate literary skill.

—Larry D. Thomas, 2008 Texas Poet Laureate and Member of the Texas Institute of Letters

Dancing on Barbed Wire is a wild, rollicking ride through some of the most imaginative fictional landscapes ever encountered. As intricate as a villanelle and yet filled with crazy and curious characters fiercely pursuing lost dreams and misplaced obsessions, this book will delight readers with both its quirky scenes and depth of passion. The trio of talented authors have created a story cycle of sixteen unforgettable tales that will pull readers in on the first page and leave them longing for more on the last page.

—Dan Williams, author of *Past Purgatory* and Director of TCU Press

This literary experiment by three long-time friends and collaborators makes for a delightful journey. The book is comprised of interlocked stories that may be enjoyed as individual fictions, some comic, some deadly serious, some edging into the mystic; but the overall effect is complex, entertaining, frequently surprising, and always thought-provoking.

—Richard Moseley, Fiction Editor, *Amarillo Bay*

Three friends, all accomplished Texas authors, sat by a campfire and dreamt up a book which is like nothing you've ever read. "A single soul in two bodies" Aristotle called friendship. *Dancing on Barbed Wire* is composed by three storytellers so in harmony with one another and their material that it feels like the work of a single soul, in token of which the tales are unattributed.

The book is ordered on a plan as complex as a sestina or the quilt of a math whiz. It stitches over lives, families, decades, and a stretch of the Lone Star State the authors know intimately, bounded by the hill country, desert plains, and Austin. There is lore topographical, agricultural and pastoral, recurring Wagnerian leitmotifs, family sagas working themselves out over years, lives that collide and connect. Characters grow familiar, change, are etched deeper, becoming ever more themselves. The book evokes cowboy songs, love spoiled and redeemed, the damage wrought by shortcomings, the entanglements of property, sex, family secrets, generations at odds. It gives us both the complaints and sweetness of the tough, persuasively conveying the points of view of children, adolescents, the middle-aged, the thoroughly aged. It has drama and suspense.

Though the tales are rooted in realities as plain as dry pastures and dead dogs, there are incursions of the magical. The effect is rich, novelistic, and not wanting for unity, though each contribution stands assertively on its own. The book winds up in a novella—jointly written, of course—that draws the collection's themes and people together, a finale that is satisfying, even optimistic, yet too honest to be called simply a happy ending.

The authors' yarn-spinning dexterity and commitment to their complicated enterprise will leave you admiring their achievement, this monument to a loved place, the human beings who occupy it, and the warm force of friendship that fuels it all.

—Robert Wexelblatt, author of Life in the *Temperate Zone* and *The Artist Wears Rough Clothing*

In this inventive collection, Jerry Craven, Andrew Geyer, and Terry Dalrymple weave together coherent, appealing stories that allow readers to focus on the intertwined narratives and to engage in untangling the mystery of which accomplished writer contributed the particular story. Tales of Texas, bastards, cats, parrots, bluebonnets, dogs, and love lost and found are woven together with barbed wire prose in this innovative approach to storytelling.

—Mark Busby, Distinguished Professor Emeritus of English, Texas State University, San Marcos; Past President, Texas Institute of Letters

Dancing on Barbed Wire

Terry Dalrymple
Jerry Craven
Andrew Geyer

edited by Tom Mack

ANGELINA
RIVER
PRESS

ISBN: 978-0-9987364-4-0
Library of Congress Control Number: 2018955092
Cover painting: based on a photograph by Todd Combs

Angelina River Press, LLC
Fort Worth, Texas

Acknowledgments

We are grateful to the editors of these journals for publishing some of the stories in this book.

Amarillo Bay
Concho River Review
descant
Langdon Review of the Literary Arts in Texas
RiverSedge
Southwestern American Literature
Writing Texas

CONTENTS

Introduction

Pity the poor short story, the sorry stepchild of the novel. It has long struggled to gain the public popularity that it deserves. There are, however, indications that its status is about to experience an upswing.

In marketing the modern short story to readers who are much more familiar with and attracted to novel-length works of fiction, writers and editors have experimented with ways to package short story collections to satisfy what appears to be the public's ingrained need for more sustained narrative. Herein lies the key question: how does one assemble a volume of tales by a single writer or an anthology of tales by multiple writers to ensure some form of internal coherence?

One solution to that dilemma is the story cycle whereby a single author produces a collection of narratives that are linked by certain unifying strategies. According to Susan Garland Mann (*The Short Story Cycle: A Genre Companion and Reference Guide*, 1989), those connecting devices may include setting, character, plot, theme, imagery, and point of view. Shared experience in combat during the Viet Nam War, for example, is what links the characters in the stories in Tim O'Brien's *The Things They Carried* (1990); the same is true for individuals of Vietnamese ancestry whose resettlement in this country is the focus of the tales in Robert Olen Butler's *A Good Scent from a Strange Mountain* (1992).

In addition to story cycles by a single writer, there have emerged more recently anthologies of tales by multiple authors, narratives connected to one another by a host of literary correspondences. *A Shared Voice* (Lamar University Press, 2013) pairs, for example, twelve tales by Texans with twelve tales by Carolinians; each pair, an anchor tale and responsive narrative, shares a literary element such as character or setting or theme. Billed as a "tapestry of tales," *A Shared Voice* offers readers a means of prolonging their reading pleasure beyond the confines of one short narrative.

The present volume provides a further variation on the anthology of linked stories. Herein three authors contribute their individual talents to the making of sixteen narratives, divided into four sections. Each of the first three is composed of four linked tales and one work of flash fiction; the fourth and final section is a novella to which all three writers contributed text.

Each of the three principal sections follows a uniform pattern. The first tale, an anchor narrative by one of the three authors, is followed by three responsive tales (one by each author) interconnecting with the others, most often by the use of linked characters, setting, plot, and theme. All four tales, the anchor narrative and the responses, conform to an internal chronology.

Those four lengthier pieces in each section are then capped by a work of flash fiction, which refers obliquely to the four stories in that unit but also links to the other short pieces that serve as codas for the three principal subsections, thus helping to weave together all of the narratives that make up the first three-quarters of the story cycle.

The fourth and final section is a novella that brings together now-familiar characters and plotlines from the first three sections and provides a satisfying conclusion to the volume as a whole. The cumulative effect of this organizational strategy is almost novelistic. Additionally, to help promote unity across the collection, the authors of the individual stories have not been identified. Each fictional narrative is listed by its title only.

Although the names of those responsible for each individual tale have been withheld in the text proper, what follows here is a key to unlocking the mystery of who wrote what. I will reveal the name of the author who contributed the anchor story in each of the three main sections. It's up to you, dear reader, to put your powers of literary analysis to the test and extrapolate from that evidence the identities of the authors of the remaining tales. In addition to one of the three anchor tales, each author penned one responsive narrative in each section, one piece of flash fiction, and one third of the concluding novella.

Jerry Craven provided the vintage tale that launches this anthology, "Sandjack Carson and the Schoolmarm." It is the anchor story for the volume's first major section entitled "Legacies of White-Hot Love."

The author of twenty-seven books to date, Jerry Craven is equally adept at writing novels, short stories, and poetry. His most recent novels include *Big Thicket, Searching for Rama's Spear, The Wild Part, Women of Thunder,* and *The Jungle's Edge.* Craven's latest foray into short fiction is entitled *Ceremonial Stones of Fire*; his most recent poetry collection is *Becoming Others.* Craven's short story "The Stone Salvation Barn" won the prestigious Frank O'Connor Award for Fiction. He serves as press director for Lamar University Literary Press and Ink Brush Press.

Andrew Geyer is responsible for "Flight," the rite-of-passage narrative that anchors the section entitled "Living in the Moment and Other Philosophies."

Andrew Geyer's tale "Fingers," the opening story in the hybrid story

14

cycle *Texas 5X5*, won the 2015 Spur Award for best short fiction from the Western Writers of America. His individually authored books include *Dixie Fish, Siren Songs from the Heart of Austin, Meeting the Dead*, and *Whispers in Dust and Bone*, which won the silver medal for best short fiction in the *Foreword Magazine* Book of the Year Awards and the 2004 Spur Award. With Tom Mack, Geyer edited the groundbreaking composite anthology *A Shared Voice*. He currently serves as Professor and Chair of English at the University of South Carolina Aiken and as fiction editor for *Concho River Review.*

Terry Dalrymple contributed the resonant anchor tale "Dead Dogs" for the final section labeled "Dead Dogs and Redemption."

A recipient of the Dr. Frances Hernandez Teacher-Scholar Award from the Conference of College Teachers of English, Terry Dalrymple holds the John S. Cargile Professorship in English at Angelo State University. Dalrymple is the founding editor of the literary journal *Concho River Review* and the author of the novel *Fishing for Trouble* and the story collections *Love Stories (Sort Of)* and *Salvation and Other Stories.* He also edited *Texas Soundtrack: Texas Stories Inspired by Texas Songs* and co-edited, with Laurence Musgrove, *Texas Weather: An Anthology of Poetry, Short Fiction, and Nonfiction.*

All three contributors to this volume have achieved recognition, both popular and critical. All three are members of the prestigious Texas Institute of Letters. As writers endowed with considerable creativity and as Texans by heritage and commitment, Craven, Dalrymple, and Geyer have lent their compelling voices to this innovative anthology focused on the people and passions of the Lone Star State.

Tom Mack, Distinguished Professor Emeritus
University of South Carolina Aiken

I. Legacies of White-Hot Love

Sandjack Carson and the Schoolmarm

Maybe the real subject is the making of the haunted house in Jasper. If so, then here is my early explanation of the cause, one signed only "Paul" and printed in the October 3, 1866 issue of *The Texas Baptist Herald*: "There appears to be a combination of causes: a young man. Romance. Novel reading. Love. Love slighted. Hopes Blighted. Then Despair. Madness. And the awful leap into eternity."

But subject and cause of themselves alone cannot tell the story. I, Paul Gruffyn Beaty, will try to do that, though the telling be difficult and fraught with guilt and blood.

The beginning might be said to be the return of Sandjack Carson, his riding into town on a hot August morning, wearing blue duckins trousers, a shirt too heavy and dark to be sensible in the East Texas summer heat, boots a Yankee soldier might have worn into battle, and a Johnny Reb cap. The minute I saw him ride past the courthouse up the Main Street hill, I knew he was heading for trouble, maybe worse than the evil he carried within him, for he surely rode toward the schoolhouse where a woman awaited, one who might make the mistake of offering him welcome, lodging, and more than lodging.

I pondered how a stealthy bullet could ward off trouble, knew myself to be the man to place such a bullet in that unwelcome rider, a single pistol shot to stop him dead. And I pondered the way of it, hiding beside Mearitt House, pushing my way with little noise among poison sumac, herbaceous vines, and low branches of loblolly pines where I might in shadows cypher a spot for death where his suspenders crossed in the back, or the front some three buttons below the neck of that heavy shirt.

The pistol waited in my saddlebag, my roan stood in front of the courthouse, so it would be an easy, but, alas, not a wise action, I warned, especially for a man of the cloth. Better to walk up the hill to Mearitt House, talk with the teacher if she would hear me, a condition I doubted, for she had determined that we never speak again. She made her pronouncement in 1861, not long after the beginning of the war. It was a dismissal of me, total and complete, though in my weakness I had thought it proper to warn her about Sandjack Carson.

That day, the day of the beginning, the day he rode into town and straight to Mearitt House, on that day I walked the hill in August heat where I caught the odor of him, a stench not unlike a piece of rotten meat. The smell greeted me before I saw him, and I wondered how the pretty girl on the porch could tolerate being that close to so foul an odor. He sat on the porch with Lucy beside him: young Lucy, beautiful Lucy who—gossip had told me—at age fifteen loved most the hours she gave to reading romance novels. She stole looks of adoration at Sandjack and he saw none of them.

But he saw me though he at first pretended otherwise in the adjusting of a shirt sleeve, a deliberate but seeming-casual untucking that revealed the derringer strapped to a wrist, a mere glimpse for me alone before hiding it again, before smiling without humor, then nodding. "Reverend Paul." He spoke more in accusation than a true greeting.

"Miss Lucy." I touched the tip of my hat. "Sandy Jack."

A malevolent frown creased his face but only for a tiny moment, then he smiled, and I knew my using his childhood name caught him off guard.

The middle must of necessity be most of a story telling the transformation of the Mearitt home—once the only schoolhouse in Jasper—into a run-down, paint-peeling, window-shattered hulk that children point to in fear and even adults whisper accusations of being that old haunted house on Main Street. Blood still, at the end of the story—if there truly be an end—clings brown and faint but visible enough, splattered darkly across boards of porch and wall beside that door through which walks no one, not since the funeral and departure of the dark woman Amanda Mearitt.

Amanda the temptress told me nothing of the ultimate violence on that porch; gossips and witnesses told me. I imagined events in that house, and I knew with certainty that the words imagination whispered in my ear were the truth of what transpired in the bedroom—all leading to what I later wrote about as that awful leap into eternity.

Demon-woman and possessed, Amanda welcomed Sandjack Carson into her bed, though that was long after I came to know her in some passionate and wrong ways.

She once visited Europe, talked of it when I went to her before the war, long before we even saw war coming, talked to me of Rome and paintings such as one in a chapel where God with flowing beard and locks pointed at Adam across a ceiling cracked by years.

"Your voice," I said, "fills with reverence when you speak of such art." It was thus in her teaching, also, a breathy tone that inspired in me some of the love for art and learning she felt with such intensity as laced

20

into the low and rich tones of her voice.

"Yes," Amanda said. "Yes." She almost whispered, and she blinked at tears, and I held her to my breast, an act that flamed both her and me into passion again when I had thought it already spent, passion that set me afire yet frightened me for such breathless and raw desire, so natural yet wrong in man, and surely it had to be rare as well as doubly wrong in woman.

After, with both of us perspiring, I pushed her aside and muttered, "Women should not behave thus." She stiffened at my words.

Her husband, she had told me, died of some mysterious fever and ague while in Rome, so Amanda made her way back to New York, then somehow to Texas and Jasper where she purchased the home she named Mearitt House, where she offered private lessons to those wanting to learn.

Her habit of speaking in low and awe-filled tones filled my breast also with awe and more, much more. I, her one adult pupil, looked into her brooding, dark eyes and saw her hunger, saw the invitation, one I yearned to enjoy even if it meant a guilty pleasure. Much of the snake lurked behind her brown eyes in her nodding toward her bedroom during that, my final lesson with the exotic schoolmarm.

The morning of that surprising resurgence of passion between us, after she stiffened and turned away, Amanda declared: "Never again."

"I can return tonight," I offered, for I believed her not at all.

"Our passion this night is good, must be good in and of itself." Her voice dropping low and warm and thick like melting wax, tones to melt me, also, so I reached for her again, but this time she pushed aside my arm.

In her dressing, silhouetted against the morning light streaming new and harsh through the window, she said, "Never again. Never, you hear? My loneliness and need cannot span the chasm you have placed between us."

"Because I am married?" I asked.

"No." She sounded angry.

"Ah. I wear the cloth. A minister should not have such feelings as you saw in me this night."

She made a gesture of annoyance, turned her face to me, her jaw set, her eyes hard. "Never again."

The guilt of that night rode me hard, and I avoided Jasper and especially Mearitt House, though I heard the gossip about the woman schoolmarm traveling to New Orleans where she married again, lived with

21

her husband for a short time before someone shot him down in an argument over a wagon. Amanda then returned to Jasper with a baby girl she and her husband had named Lucy.

I fled, moved west with wife and young son, moved to a church in Austin and a parsonage surrounded by a barbed wire fence, called a *bob war* fence by the locals. In that scruffy part of the state the trees I loved so in East Texas grew scant, most replaced with greenery hardly worthy of the name *trees*. Most were stumpy and mean, mesquite armed with needles, shrubs rather than real trees with thorns in abundance to remind me of a crown of thorns, tiny trees that bespoke punishment I deserved but did not earn. In Austin for years I preached the Word with fervor, prayed in private for absolution, and came to forget, mostly, that one night in Mearitt House when I briefly became someone else and saw in a woman such wild darkness as I had never suspected any woman capable of having within her. Dangerous. Born of the serpent.

Then the war loomed and the relative safety of East Texas grew in appeal for its isolation from the possible madness of battle. The Lord called me to Bevilport, so with wife and son I returned to preach again in the Piney Woods. There the story of Mearitt House resumed in a most unexpected way after my son, grown into a young man while in Austin, gunned down a Bevilport lumberjack and fled to Jasper where he somehow found refuge in the home of Amanda Mearitt.

This son, who had come much to deny my authority over him, had grown tall, handsome, and cruel. To my mind the only characteristic that clung to him from childhood was his unruly shock of sand-colored hair, hair which earned him the name his mother and I called him. He proclaimed he hated his childhood name, and after he killed a man and fled, he changed his name to Sandjack Carson.

When I found him hiding a mere ten miles from Bevilport, I wanted to tell him to turn himself over to the law, yet he being my son, I could not bear the realization that what awaited him was the noose, for Texas courts make an abundant use of hanging. So I counseled him to join the army, to go to war, for that way he could avoid justice and perhaps survive.

He and I sat on the porch, the same one that later, after the war, became splattered with blood. I thought in those moments that he had the foul odor of evil about him. He wore the same shirt, dark and heavy, that he had worn the day he committed his murder, and I had the illusion that he had never washed it, had never shifted into another shirt, which would explain the rank smell emitting from him, though I still believed it was the stench of evil.

He listened to my counsel, then in that meanness of spirit he developed in leaving childhood, he showed me the hole in his shirt sleeve, rolled up the sleeve to reveal the derringer he had strapped to his arm, explained the wire mechanism he used to fire a bullet by raising his arm and twisting his shoulders. "The man picked on me, and not for the first time. But that last time, when he called me names I could not abide, I thought myself ready until he struck me to the ground." Sandy spoke in words ringing with pride and triumph, he sitting on the porch in much the same place where I later found him sitting beside pretty Lucy as she looked at him with childish adoration. "When I got to my feet and raised my arm, the bully rogue took the stance of a man expecting fisticuffs. That's when I twisted to pull the wire and fire the pistol that shot this hole through my sleeve."

"And murdered a man," I said.

"No. I killed a man who needed killing. You taught me that murder is wrong." He looked at me with all the contempt of youth.

"Join the army." I made no attempt to hide my shock and anger. "Join. Live through the war if you must, then never return to East Texas."

He laughed harsh and cruel and nodded toward the door of Mearitt House. "But that schoolmarm has taught me much, both during the days and at night, so of course I will return, for I would marry her, would stay with her. Forever."

I knew in that moment I had lost my son to evil. Even if I did not wish him to hang for his first fatal misdeed, perhaps I might be wishing for him to hang for his second, the bedding of Amanda.

At that moment she came to the door. "You must leave, Paul. These are my final words to you. Leave."

"She stole your soul," I said. The sadness of such loss washed over me, a forever loss to me and worse to him. Did any man deserve to have woman heap such wickedness upon him? "You must," I said to Amanda, "beware of this man, for now he is evil."

As I departed I marveled at my own counsel, telling a woman to beware the evil in a man who possessed evil because she conjured it into him.

Sandy Jack Beaty, wearing his new name Sandjack Carson, went to war, survived, and somehow chose to return on the very day I had Bevilport business in the Jasper County courthouse and thus experienced the misfortune of seeing him ride into town and up the hill. It was an inauspicious day when I walked with misgivings to Mearitt House, the day Sandy showed me in his war-hardened bravado that derringer he still kept on his arm, no doubt with intent to murder again.

Lucy stood with proper respect when her mother came to the door. The schoolmarm spoke to Sandjack, not to me. "Does the Reverend Paul," she asked in a flat tone, "have something to say to me?"

I refused to look at her. "Sandy, tell this woman *no*." I stood to leave but on impulse turned and looked full into her dark eyes. "This man, Sandjack Carson, is even more dangerous than he was before he went to war. Beware. Beware."

Amanda laughed too loud, too high-pitched for the laughter to be born of amusement. Lucy stepped back and looked puzzled, and Sandjack smiled, toothy, mean. I left that terrible house, returned to the courthouse, then rode the ten miles home.

It happened two days later, and the story of the gunshot at Mearitt House traveled fast. Many claimed the event was reported accurately, for three young scholars witnessed it: Lucy walking through the front door to confront Sandjack Carson on the porch. She said something to him, and he scowled, then shook his head. Lucy sighed loud and miserable, took a pistol from her apron, put the barrel into her mouth, and pulled the trigger.

The end came with horrid and sudden violence, the end for Lucy, the end for whatever sordid bond Sandjack and Amanda had between them, and the end of the first Jasper schoolhouse, for after Amanda left, it changed into a haunted house no one would ever again wish to call home.

Amanda moved away after the funeral to vanish from my life except for a single letter she sent to me two years later. No one ever heard what became of Sandjack Carson, and Mearitt House tumbled into disrepair, into entropy, into a place to be avoided and feared and talked about only in hushed whispers. The ending of the story of the house was hardly sudden but ongoing for years.

Amanda's letter was short, cryptic, painful. "I apologize," it said, "for never telling you about Lucy's father."

Bastard Children

"Last lover," Augie Winston said. "What was his name?"

"Why that?" Lily said and tapped his shoulder with a fist.

"Why not?" He kissed her, just a peck on the lips.

They had spent a quiet evening together, he grilling pork chops, she preparing dirty rice and a garden salad. He finished off two glasses of Merlot during dinner and began a third on the living room couch, light jazz playing in the background. Lily still nursed her first glass. They began a round of Truth or Dare. By the time Augie asked for Lily's last lover's name, they had already dared each other into nudity. Augie, knowing all the dares would involve sexual foreplay, had chosen dares wholeheartedly. Lily, on the other hand, enjoyed postponing the inevitable, enjoyed the tease, and so had chosen truth every other time or so.

"Okay," she said. "Jasper. His name was Jasper."

Augie tilted his back and laughed. "Jasper! What was he, a Kentucky pig farmer?"

She slapped his chest and giggled. "You're terrible."

"And you," he said, "made up that name." He clutched her hand and stood up. "Come with me, young lady. You owe me a dare."

"It's really his name," she said. But she still stood, giggling, and followed him to the bedroom.

Afterwards, the two of them tangled together in exquisite exhaustion, she placed a finger against his lips and said, "Hey, want to know something true?"

He smiled, eyes closed. "What?"

"I'm pregnant."

His eyes popped open. "Pregnant?"

"Yeah. You know, with child. *Your* child."

He bolted upright in bed. "Oh, shit!" He slapped both palms over his face, and his mind scrambled for a better response.

She rolled away, her back to him. "I thought you'd be happy," she said quietly.

Happy? he thought. Why would she think he'd be happy?

"Listen," he said, "have you thought about...." He stopped himself before saying the word. He should do the right thing. He should say he was happy. He should offer to marry her. "Well, you know, have you thought about alternatives?"

"Alternatives?" She rolled back toward him and glared. "Jesus,

Augie, you're such a bastard."

And he was. He was a bastard, and she knew it, knew that both his father and his mother had been absent for all of his twenty-four years. And in those years all he'd ascertained about them was that his father had worked construction in Odessa and had sex with a nineteen-year-old girl, a waitress in a greasy spoon called Good Eats, before moving on to some other job in some other town. When Augie was born, the waitress had entrusted him to a friend, another waitress at Good Eats, who had seen to it that he was safely delivered to a Catholic home for infants and children in San Antonio.

Jesus, what did he know about parenting? He'd never known anything but group homes until he'd run away at sixteen. Then he had managed, at times just barely, to stay within the law as he scrounged a living. Eventually, a man he knew only as Jake taught him some carpentry when they worked together on a house construction, and he had managed to improve those skills until he made a decent living in the home-building business in Fort Worth.

And then he met Lily, a drive-up bank teller with a beautiful smile, a quirky sense of humor, a tender heart, and an appetite for explosive sex.

She had turned her bare back to him again. He glanced at her smooth skin, placed his palm against her spine. "Okay. Just let me think."

The next morning, overnight bag tossed next to him on the seat, he drove south in a Ford F-150 that had seen better days but that still got him where he needed to go. And where he needed to go right now was simply away, somewhere he could clear his head, work this fatherhood thing out in a reasonable way. Maybe Galveston, he thought, since he was headed south anyway. A little sun, surf, and sand might be just the thing to clarify his muddied thoughts.

Somewhere around Centerville, a woman's voice, loud and clear and demanding, said, "Jasper!" He flinched, glanced across at the passenger side. Was it Lily's voice? She had said her last lover's name was Jasper. But the voice seemed deeper than hers, more seasoned. A subconscious voice of his own, maybe. But why so demanding?

By the time he passed Madisonville, Augie had mostly recovered from the shock, and instead of the voice, ran his fatherhood dilemma through his mind again and again without resolution.

"Jasper!" the voice said again near the exit for U.S. 190. Augie again convulsed and again checked the passenger seat. Then, without fully knowing why, he flipped on his blinker and veered onto the exit a sign promised would take him east to Jasper.

A kid. Damn, this was not what he expected at twenty-four. What did he know about kids? Well, what he did know was that a kid should not be fatherless as he was. On the other hand, because he was fatherless, what did he know about fathering? The tapes reran themselves time and again in his head, but the result remained the same: terror at the thought of fatherhood and crushing guilt at the thought of deserting fatherhood. What merit was there in foregoing the fatherhood that terrified him? On the other hand, what merit was there in accepting the consequences of his actions and most likely failing miserably at parenthood? By the time he reached Martin Dies, Jr. State Park and crossed the lake, he had progressed many miles, but he had reached no mental or emotional destination.

A few miles farther on, he spotted the sign for Jasper and turned onto US Highway 96 North. Before he'd gone two hundred yards, another sign with an arrow pointing west drew his attention: "Mearitt House Bed and Breakfast."

What merit was there? Well, there was the Mearitt House. The day had been plenty strange already; why not keep it up? He turned left onto the narrow two-lane, pine-lined road and followed signs toward the B&B. Perhaps a mile later, he turned onto a sandy driveway and approached a small white house with blue eaves. Nestled amongst the tall pines, it looked too small to serve as a B&B, but the sign by the front-yard gate said otherwise.

A dark-skinned woman answered his knock. "Ms. Mearitt?" he asked.

She laughed. "Lord, no, child. Was I Ms. Mearitt I'd be white and over a hundred and twenty years old."

"Is this the B&B?"

"Come on in." She swung the screen open and gestured for him to pass through. "Mearitt House an old name," she said. "Story says a girl killed herself in the house. Fell into disrepair long many year ago. Some old crazy man tore it down and used the lumber to build this house here." She clutched Augie's elbow and guided him into the den, crowded with old but plush chairs and a sofa, the walls home to dozens of what appeared to be very old photographs. "Sit, child, sit." She nodded to the sofa and he sat. "Old man claimed it was haunted and just up and left." She eased into a wingback chair across from him. "It sat empty until I bought it from the city in nineteen and ninety-four." She suddenly threw up her hands. "But, good Lord, that's more than you want to know. You need a room?"

Before answering, he considered her voice, its solid, strong tone. Was hers the voice he had heard in the truck? He couldn't be sure, but that possibility made no sense anyway. He studied her closely. Definitely mid-fifties. Dark, smooth skin. Dark hair falling in waves over her shoulders. Dark, somehow deep eyes, and a perfect complexion but for a small scar on the right side of her chin. She smiled warmly.

"Yes, ma'am, I guess I do," he said.

"Oh, child, don't call me ma'am. My name Sybil, you call me that." She leaned forward, reached across, and squeezed his hand. "You just call me Sybil." Her touch was warm, somehow familiarly soft and comforting.

"Sybil," he said. "Yes, I'd like a room."

She smiled, released his hand, and stood up. "Back of the house is yours. Bedroom, bathroom, and sitting room. Hundred and nine a night for the comfortablest bed and the biggest, most tastiest warm breakfast in the whole county."

"I'll get my bag."

At the truck, he retrieved his phone and texted Lily: *I'm okay. I love you. Really.*

Sybil offered him a dinner of leftovers. As they ate warmed meatloaf, mashed potatoes, and homemade bread slathered with real butter, she asked, "Somebody send you here?"

He coughed, sipped his sweet tea. "Not exactly."

She paused, a forkful of potatoes near her lips. "Uh-huh." She took the bite, swallowed. "What your real name?"

"I told you. Augie Winston."

"No, child, I mean your *real* name."

He coughed again. "Are you a witch or something?"

"Witch!" She chuckled. "Aw, hell no. I just know things. Don't know how I know, but I do."

Augie set his fork on his plate, sipped more sweet tea. "I grew up in homes. You know, for unwanted kids. They called me Billy Smith."

Sybil looked at his face, cocked her head to the right, then to the left. "No, you not Billy Smith. That not your real name."

Augie shrugged. "Don't know if I ever had one. But when I ran away, I called myself Augie because of that character, you know, Augie March. And I called myself Winston because that's what I smoked."

Sybil laughed a big, hearty laugh, but then her smile faded and her face turned serious. "Okay, Augie Winston, you listen to Sybil. Your parents sorry for what they done. And they sorry for your troubled time, too." She stretched her long, slender arms across the table and patted his hand.

"Doubtful," he said, and then the full significance of her words hit him. "What time of trouble?"

Sybil raised her eyebrows. "Why, this one, child."

"Who says I'm troubled?"

"Oh, you definitely troubled."

He shivered but let the topic drop.

His bed, as promised, was immensely comfortable. Despite his tumbled thoughts he slept soundly until about two a.m., when he awoke disturbed by dream images. In one, Lily stood, hands folded over a hugely swollen belly, and simply stared at him with sad, bloodshot eyes. In the other, four people stood at the foot of his bed and pointed accusing fingers at him. He recognized none of them and yet three looked vaguely familiar: a blonde teenaged girl, a blonde man with stringy, dirty hair, and a blonde girl of five or six whose hair also looked dirty and unkempt. The fourth was the oldest, a dark-headed woman with fiery eyes.

He slept fitfully after that. When he awoke a little after eight, he splashed his face with water, slipped on jeans and a tee-shirt. He considered calling Lily but decided otherwise. He had come to no decision, and as for any other conversation, what would he say? How could he explain why he was where he was when he didn't even know that answer himself? He dropped his phone on the bed and followed his nose to the kitchen. Breakfast, again as promised, was huge and hot. He sipped steaming coffee and gorged on sausage links, bacon, fluffy scrambled eggs, biscuits and gravy, and finished with a side of fresh blueberries, strawberries, and sliced bananas. He leaned back in his chair, held his stomach with both hands, and laughed for the first time since he and Lily had played Truth or Dare.

"Miss Sybil, you do make a damn fine breakfast."

She laughed with him. "I do what I can." She looked down into the steam rising from her coffee and stirred slowly. "So, you sleep okay?"

He dodged a direct answer. "The bed was great."

"Uh-huh," she said. "So no bad dreams?"

Witch, he thought, but he nodded. "Couple."

"'Bout what?"

"A dark-haired woman, a blonde girl, a scruffy blonde man, and little girl, also blonde."

Sybil paused, a spoonful of blueberries near her lips. She set the spoon back into her bowl. "Good Lord, son, you dreaming history."

"History?"

She arose and turned to the wall behind her. "Look here," she said. He joined her, facing the wall of old photographs. She pointed. "That the woman you saw last night?"

A dark-headed woman stood on the front porch of a house, a lighter-haired girl to her left. Augie stepped closer, peered at their faces. "I think so," he said. "And the girl, too."

"That woman, Amanda Mearitt, she owned this house back in the late nineteenth century before it was tore down and rebuilt here where we standing. That teenaged girl, she was Ms. Mearitt's daughter by a preacher man sleeping with her out of wedlock. Story says he never knew about her till after she shot herself dead." Sybil stepped around Augie to another photo. "And that man there is Sandjack Carson, most likely who you saw last night, too."

Engrossed, Augie studied that photo even more closely than the first. The man stood with two others, all with their hands in their coat pockets, all unsmiling in front of what appeared to be a saloon.

"He was that preacher man's legitimate son," Sybil added.

"He looks sort of familiar."

Sybil waved his comment off. "Likely just because you saw the pictures while eating last night."

Augie scrambled to remember the pictures from the evening before. He had noticed the number of pictures on the walls, of course, but he couldn't recall looking closely at any of them. Then again, he had sat across from Sybil, facing that wall. He might have noticed them without registering what he saw.

Sybil pushed back from the table. "Come walk with me. It's a fine June morning."

He followed her out the back door, across a creaky wooden porch, down two steps, and into sunlight just beginning to pierce the pines and warm the mild June morning.

She walked briskly ahead. "Got nearly four acres here," she narrated. "Try to keep it as wild as possible, the way the Lord meant."

Augie stayed several paces behind, his progress slowed by pauses to study the black earth and the underbrush or to look up at the tips of the pines stretching toward sun light. "It's nice," he said. "Kind of peaceful." She had moved several steps farther ahead. He took long strides to catch up. "Sybil, that little girl I saw, do you know about her?"

"Not really, child. But was I to guess I'd say she was Sandjack's daughter." They followed a path of sorts that wound around her property. "Story says he raped a woman down in South Texas, had a daughter he never even knew about."

"Amanda Mearitt's daughter, Sandjack Carson's daughter, and me." He kicked at the sandy path. "Damn bastard children everywhere."

Sybil slipped her arm around his at the elbow. "In that regard, child, you nothing new in this world." She stared intently at the side of his face, her deep, dark eyes pained. "Damn shame, isn't it?"

They passed into a narrow clearing shin-deep in wild grasses. "Do you have children, Sybil?"

She paused, sucked in her breath. "Oh, look there." She raised her arm, pointed a long, slender brown finger. "See that flower there, the little purple one peeking through the grass? Called a pine woods lily. Not many around here. Rare. Precious."

He humored her, looked at the flower. "Yes, it's pretty."

"Not really a lily," she said. "Iris, I think. But still lovely. Lily a good name."

Lily a good name. Rare. Precious. A witch, Augie thought. She's definitely a witch.

Sybil pulled her attention from the flower and began walking again. They made small talk the rest of the way, mostly about plants and flowers she pointed out, and once about a wolf spider that skittered across the path in front of them. Augie half-listened, his head full of Lily and bastard children. Back at the house, Sybil began clearing the table. When he tried to help, she brushed his hand away. "This my job," she said. While she worked, he wandered the room, looking at the many old photographs hanging there.

"You know where I got those?" Sybil said. She stood in the kitchen doorway drying her hands on a dish towel.

Augie smirked. "You were there, right?"

She grinned. "Child, you still on the witch stuff?"

"Maybe a little," he said. But he, too, grinned. "Where did you get them?"

"Library. They not originals, just copies. Originals in the library." She turned back into the kitchen. "Oh, yes, lots of information in the library."

And suddenly he knew what he would do the rest of the day.

31

With Sybil's precise directions, he easily found Water Street and located the library. The librarian he talked with, a woman in her sixties named Joan, knew only what Sybil knew about Sandjack Carson and knew nothing about his alleged illegitimate daughter. She suggested a genealogy web site, but he found there no references to any Sandjack Carson. He switched to the library's electronic catalogue, found nothing of use, and began searching for Texas public records, 1880-1910. Eventually, he focused on South Texas, where he found a brief note about someone named Elena Esquivel giving birth to a "girlchild" in Laredo on August 9, 1890. Child's name: Rosa. Father's name: unknown. That was the best he had to go on, but it turned up little until he happened across a 1907 San Antonio news bit about a woman named Rosa Escovido who had jumped to her death from a seedy hotel's second-story window. A newborn child had been found in her room, father, again, unknown. It was a stretch, but the woman's first name was right, and her last name was vaguely similar, perhaps a name the bastard child Rosa had assumed. Her abandoned bastard child had been taken in by an otherwise childless couple, Jeremy and Martha Smith, who named the boy William. *Smith*. The name Augie had until he changed it himself. He kept digging.

At six o'clock, Joan the librarian said they were closing and he would have to go. By then he had managed to piece together what he thought, sketchy as the evidence was, might be his own lineage. If he was right, his lineage began with Sandjack Carson, his great-great-great grandfather, whose own father had a bastard child, the girl who killed herself; Rosa Esquivel/Escovido followed, a bastard child who bore another bastard child, William Smith, who had a family of his own but who had also fathered a child with a whore, a child he never claimed; that child, Gregory Smith, perhaps Augie's grandfather, had deserted his second cousin when she claimed he impregnated her; she bore a child named Stephen Meyers-Smith, the man Augie suspected might be his own father. Augie felt, in short, that if the genealogy were accurate, he was a bastard child resulting from a long line of bastard children.

In his truck outside the library, he slumped, forehead pressed against the steering wheel. If all this were true—and he admitted to himself that it might well not be—he should break the bastard child curse, should marry Lily, should be a father to their child. But if it were true, what kind of father would he be, given his bloodline, given the genes that possibly predisposed him to desert, to leave children behind, to deny responsibility? Would he end up making matters worse by attempting to own up and failing in the attempt?

He drove aimlessly, not ready to discuss his findings with Sybil, who'd surely ask questions. Mostly, he wanted to talk with Lily, tell her what he found, ask her what she thought. But he knew, already, what she would say. She'd say she didn't care about his family history, she cared about him. She'd say his research was sketchy, anyway, that he'd made really tenuous connections among the scattered bits of information he'd found. She'd say she wanted him with her, raising their child. He wasn't ready to hear that, wasn't ready to decide.

When he passed a place called Martin's Mexican Restaurant, he realized he hadn't eaten since breakfast, and he pulled into the parking lot. He focused little on the taste of the food but thought it decent enough Tex-Mex. The cold beer interested him more, and he ordered a second before finishing the combination dinner. Then he ordered a third and a fourth, hoping to wash all of the questions out of his mind.

He arrived at the Mearitt House B&B about ten-thirty. Sybil, apparently, had gone to bed but left the door unlocked. He locked it, turned out lights, and fell onto his bed fully clothed. He dreamed of Lily and of bastard children and of a witch named Sybil. He awoke just before nine, groaned, stumbled to the bathroom. He considered plopping back into bed, but lured by the aroma of another big breakfast, he headed toward the dining room.

An off-white envelope set next to his plate contained a note from Sybil: *Errands. Will be gone all day. Coffee in the pot, breakfast in the oven. Bill enclosed.* He slipped the bill from the envelope, unfolded it. Underneath the Mearitt House B&B letterhead, she had written, *Amount owed: Do the right thing.*

What did Sybil know, and how the hell did she know what she knew? Or did she know nothing? Was her seeming clairvoyance just another figment of his imagination, like the voice he had heard in his truck? And what about his research, those sketchy connections Lily would have pointed out? Were they yet another figment? Had he jumped to conclusions too quickly?

Augie poured a cup of coffee in the kitchen and carried it out onto the rickety porch. He sat on the top step and stared out toward Sybil's property. He wondered how many pine woods lilies bloomed out there. Sybil had said they bloomed only in the morning. He thought about Lily, blooming with pregnancy. "Do the right thing," Sybil had said. But what, really, was the right thing? Maybe he'd stay here for a while, find out what

33

Sybil really did know about him. Maybe he'd go on to Galveston, but he doubted that sun, surf, and sand would clear his head any better. Maybe he'd go home to Lily, talk with her at least. But a future with her and a child still terrified him. Maybe he should let that child live as happily as possible with its mother, undisturbed by the influence of a man who knew nothing about being a father, a bastard from a long line of bastards. But he hated the thought of being a coward, hated even more the thought of never seeing Lily again.

His coffee had cooled beside him on the step. He carried it inside, dumped it, rinsed the cup, and then went to his bedroom to pack. He had, at least, eliminated one possibility. He would not stay there and wait for Sybil. On U.S. 190 a mile or two from I-45, the voice spoke again, the same voice he had heard before. "Right thing," it said, and again he couldn't tell whether it was in his head or in the air. Was it Sybil's voice? Lily's? A figment of his own? He pulled onto the shoulder.

"What is the right thing?" he yelled at the bodiless voice, but it provided no answer. South on I-45 would lead to Galveston; north on I-45, to Fort Worth and Lily and his unborn child. He stared out the window, watched cars whiz past, and thought. Finally, he nodded, pulled back onto pavement, and drove toward the interstate.

Troubadours

It isn't just the fact that she's a stranger.

No, the fracking boom that's fired up on the Eagle Ford Shale, and the building boom that followed, have brought a lot of unfamiliar faces to Jordan. And I couldn't be happier to see them. A lot of the roughnecks and construction workers come into the Second Chance Café. I serve the best chili in Southwest Texas, in three varieties—a three-alarm shredded beef with fiery red peppers, a two-alarm ground venison with jalapenos, and a one-alarm ground beef and pinto beans with mild green chiles—with thick slices of homemade sourdough bread on the side. There are half-pound burgers and wedge fries, chicken fried steaks, spicy catfish stew, spicy-battered fried catfish filets with hushpuppies, and ice-cold beer to wash it all down. I serve the beer and run the register, hire perky girls from Jordan High School to serve the food, and the hungry young men come in droves. But that doesn't explain the dark-haired woman in the corner, casing the place with nervous eyes.

I noticed something odd about this particular stranger the minute she walked in out of the seething summer air lugging a black backpack in front of her instead of clutching a purse at her side, as if trying to hide the baby bump I spotted in an instant. She lowered herself carefully into the corner chair at table 15, ordered decaf coffee and a water, asked for the Wi-Fi password, and started watching everything that went on. No small-talk, not even a hello—which was unusual in and of itself in a little town like Jordan—and with a jittery edge in her voice, along with an undertone of something else. Hostility? Secrecy?

Something. Enough to set off a blip on my people radar.

As the restaurant filled and emptied with a mix of roughnecks in dirty coveralls and locals herding kids—Beau and Wanda Mulebach were among them, rocking their brand-new baby son in his car seat carrier in the booth at 25—the skittish stranger kept her back against the wall, her baby bump beneath the table, and her backpack at her feet. She drank decaf and water but ate nothing, seemingly absorbed in her cell phone but glancing up every time someone walked in, and eyeing the other customers and me around the edge of her phone screen.

Now it's after ten. I've already flipped the OPEN sign in the window that faces the state highway around to CLOSED, and let Lydia Rodriquez, the head cook, and Jenny Thompson, the late-shift waitress, go home. The only people left in the Second Chance Café are myself, standing guard at the cash register, and the dark-haired woman in the corner with the unpaid check for her coffee face-down on the table.

"Ma'am," I say at last, "I'm going to have to ask you to settle up. The café closed at 9:30, and it's 10:15."

Instead of replying, the woman starts tapping with both thumbs on her cell phone screen, rapid-fire.

"Ma'am?"

The only answer is more tapping, and the echo of my voice off the green-and-white checkered floor tiles.

I'm not the jumpy type, but I've taken in two thousand dollars tonight if I've taken in a dime, and the roughnecks and construction workers mostly pay cash. The pregnant woman's baby daddy could be lurking outside like a wolf spider ready to burst into the café and shove a gun into my face. And the state highway that bisects downtown Jordan runs straight down to Eagle Pass and Piedras Negras, so the pair could be in Mexico inside of an hour.

When the woman reaches into her backpack and starts fumbling around with something bulky, the blip on my people radar balloons to fill the entire screen. I snatch the telephone off the counter, start dialing Jim Thompson's personal cell—Jim is Jenny Thompson's father, chief deputy at the sheriff's office that's just a block away—and glance over into the corner, certain that I'll see the business end of a pistol pointing back at me.

But what the dark-haired woman holds instead is a black leather wallet. Empty, from the blank way she's staring down into it. Tears are streaming down her cheeks. And it comes to me as I set the receiver back into its cradle that the emotion I heard in her voice earlier, underneath the jittery edge, wasn't hostility or secrecy. It was heartbreak. The rush of relief that comes hard on the heels of that realization fades slowly into sympathy. I walk to the waitstation, pour myself a cup of high octane, and carry both coffee pots over to the corner table.

"Do you mind if I join you?" I ask.

"Are you the manager?"

"Manager. Cook. Cashier. Bartender." I pull out a chair and sit down. "I own the place. Although sometimes it feels more like the place owns me."

"I can't pay you for the coffee," the woman sniffles.

"I kind of figured that," I say gently, "from the look on your face when you opened your wallet." I know enough about heartbreak not to mention the tears that are dripping now from the woman's chin down onto

36

her wrinkled shirt. "Can you sing?"

"Excuse me?"

"In the Middle Ages, there were poets who traveled the South of France singing songs about courtly love in return for their room and board. They called themselves *troubadours*." I reach the decaf pot over, refill the woman's cup. "I thought maybe ..."

"I'm afraid I don't sing very well. And I don't really know much about poetry."

"Me either. But I've traveled the South of France. My favorite place was Cannes on the Cote D'Azur." I sip my coffee, a rich French roast ground fresh from beans I have custom-roasted at a shop called the Mystic Café on the San Antonio River Walk. "After my husband died, it was my lifetime goal to retire there and open a restaurant on the Boulevard de la Croisette just off the beach. I was going to call the place the Café le Coq after my late husband—his nickname was Rooster—and there was going to be a big red neon gamecock out front that would be visible a mile out at sea." I feel myself smile, thinking about Rooster and about the turquoise water and powdery sand. "I opened the Second Chance Café here in Jordan instead."

"I don't understand."

"I guess what I'm trying to say is that sometimes things don't work out like we planned. And that can be okay."

"I don't ... I don't know what I'm ..." The silent tears become choking sobs. "I just feel hollowed-out."

I fetch a cloth napkin and hand it to the woman. "Sometimes the troubadours told stories of their travels instead of singing. So tell me: How long has it been since you ate a meal?"

"I had a box of Triscuits this morning. The chili pepper thin crisps."

"Hmm ... So you like spicy?"

The woman nods.

"The kitchen is closed for the night, but I can feed you a bowl of the best chili in Southwest Texas. How does that sound?"

"But I don't have any money. And the credit card company just cancelled my account."

"Tell me your story instead. You can start with your name."

"I'm Lily," the woman says, meeting my eyes for the first time.

"Howdy, Lily. I'm May Belle Stiles. That wasn't so hard, was it? And what's his name?"

"His?"

37

I glance pointedly at the baby bump that's pressing against the wooden tabletop.

"Augie," Lily says and the sobs start again. "His ... name is ..."

"Augie? Well, that's a beginning. You still owe me a middle and an end. But let's get some food in you first." I lead Lily back to the kitchen, heat a bowl of the one-alarm chili in the microwave, butter a thick slice of sourdough bread. Then we walk back out to the corner table, and I sip coffee while Lily wolfs her meal.

"I didn't realize how hungry I was until I started eating," she says, swabbing the bottom of the bowl with the last bit of bread. "Thank you. That's the best chili I've ever had."

"I make it myself," I say, frankly pleased, as I top off our cups. "I'm more partial to the three-alarm recipe, but the one-alarm is probably better on an empty belly. Now that you've finished, I'd like to hear the rest of the story. Your name is Lily, and his name is Augie. Why don't we pick up from there?"

"Augie and I met in Fort Worth, which is where I'm from, and we fell in love. Anyway, I thought we were in love. Every minute we didn't spend at work, we spent together. Then I got pregnant. And he left."

"So you followed him?"

Lily shakes her head. "Not at first. Augie grew up in an orphanage and in foster homes—his mother gave him up—and when I told him about our baby, he said he needed to get out of town for a few days and think the whole fatherhood thing through. He texted me the next day and told me that he loved me. Then he called from Jasper, in middle-of-nowhere East Texas, and we talked. He said he was on his way back to Fort Worth, that he was ready to give family life a try." The tears start to flow again. "That was two months ago."

"He never showed up in Fort Worth?"

"No. But he's still paying his rent. The man who owns the house Augie lives in, and who introduced Augie and me, is an old friend of my family. He lives right across the street. He'd tell me if Augie came home."

I find myself studying Lily. She's young—early twenties, I guess—and thin, naturally pretty, with pale delicate skin and a fiery intensity in her eyes despite the tears. She reminds me of myself thirty years ago. Wild. And crazy in love with Rooster. I'll never forget the way I felt when I lost him. Heartbroken. Hollowed-out.

"I was born in Jasper," I say, "and I spent my girlhood there, before my father came to Jordan for the last oil boom. The thing I remember most, besides all the pine trees, was a parrot named Pal. He belonged to a retired sea captain who lived next door, and he would perch in a chinaberry tree in the front yard every morning and curse the mailman. It was only the mailman he cursed. I never understood why."

"The captain probably had credit card bills," Lily says. "I've cursed the mailman once or twice myself." For the first time since she walked into the Second Chance Café, she smiles. "I was in Jasper last week. I found the bed and breakfast Augie stayed in. The lady who owns the place remembered him. She said he'd gone to the library to try and track down his family."

"What in the world led you here? I'm guessing you didn't come to Jordan for the oil boom."

"After Jasper, I drove to San Antonio, to the orphanage Augie grew up in. He'd been there and looked through their records. He searched through the files at the county courthouse too. Augie works in the construction business. He's a subcontractor, a framer, and I figured he'd need money. So I checked with the big home construction companies. Turns out he'd worked as a framer for Toll Brothers. A guy he crewed with said that Augie had a contract to do framework on one of the hotels they're building here in Jordan." Lily fiddles with her cell phone, then reaches it across the table. "That's Augie. He hasn't been in here, has he? This is the kind of place he likes."

I look at the photo on Lily's cell phone. The man I see is lean and dark-haired, with green eyes and a strong jaw, his skin darkly tanned from working in the Texas sun. He looks an awful lot like Rooster, and I feel a stab of pain in my chest—the same mix of longing and of loss that I felt a week and a half ago when Augie first walked into the Second Chance Café and ordered coffee and breakfast tacos, which I serve from 6-9 a.m. He's been in every morning since, except for Sunday when the restaurant is closed.

I shift my eyes carefully from the photo to the eager look on Lily's face. "Sorry," I say at last, shaking my head for emphasis. Then I look back at the phone. "Arthur has a cell phone just like that. I don't have much use for one myself."

"Arthur?"

"Arthur is my partner."

"Is he here?" There is pleading in Lily's voice now. "Could I ask him if he's seen Augie?"

"Arthur doesn't work in the restaurant. We own the building

together, and he runs the antique shop next door. He's kind of a silent partner, I guess. In more ways than one." I pause, lock my eyes onto Lily's. "But before we get to the end of your story, there's a question I need you to answer: What are you hoping to get from this man who keeps running away from you?"

"Love," Lily says, glancing down into her cup. "What else?"

"How about a father for your child? A life partner. Someone you can count on not to go hopscotching across Texas the minute things get tough. What if Augie can't give you any of those things?"

"But he can! When Augie took me out on our first date, instead of dinner and a movie, he took me swimming and hiking at Cedar Hills State Park. It was early spring, and we were driving out there in Augie's old Ford truck with the windows down. All of a sudden he pulled over to the side of the road and bounded out of the truck into a field of bluebonnets." Still staring down into her decaf, Lily half-smiles, as though she can see the memory reflected on the dark surface. "He picked an armload of flowers—as many as he could hold—and stood there grinning back at the truck until I got out and walked over to him. Then he handed me this mass of bluebonnets, and as our arms linked around the flowers, he kissed me for the first time. And I knew, right there and then, that he was the one. It wasn't just the flowers and the kiss. It was the promise of that kind of life, and that kind of love, you know? Full of grand romantic gestures. I knew I'd spend the rest of my life loving Augie."

I have to press my lips tight together to keep from saying what I'm thinking. Except for the baby bump, when I look at Lily, I see myself thirty years ago. Loving Rooster. I remember the peaks and valleys of our fiery, turbulent, cut-short married life—full of grand romantic gestures—and although the peaks were incredible, I've learned enough about living to know now that the valleys were deeper. And the financial hole Rooster left me in when he died from an early heart attack took me the better part of three decades of hard work to dig out of.

"And if the love isn't still there?" I ask finally. "Or if you can't find him?"

Lily starts to take a sip of decaf, hesitates, puts the cup back on the table. "How far is it to Laredo from here?"

"A couple of hours, depending on how fast you drive. You're a lot closer to Piedras Negras than you are to Nuevo Laredo, if you aim to cross the Rio Grande. Why?"

"I'm thinking of disappearing. Just crossing the river and keeping on going. If Augie won't have me, I've got no place to go."

"What about your parents?"

"They won't even speak to me. And anyway, I don't want my parents. I want Augie."

I reach across the table and pat Lily's hand that feels slender and delicate, a child's hand. "Do you have a place to stay the night?"

"I was planning to sleep in my car."

"You sit right here while I put these dishes away and rinse out the coffee pots. Then you can come home with me. I have a spare room you can stay in for tonight, and maybe—just maybe—tomorrow will take care of itself. In the meantime, there's something I'd like you to see."

I shut down the restaurant and lock the front door, then we walk to our cars and I lead Lily through downtown Jordan, past the post office and the historic courthouse that hulks like a castle in the light of the full moon that is rising, and out South Prospect Street to my house on the edge of town. Arthur has left the porch light on, but the moon blazing just above the tops of the mesquites lights the low ranch-style house and the close-cropped grass and the ocotillo that is in full bloom as I lead Lily up the sidewalk—she's pulling a suitcase with wheels—and across the front porch into the living room.

I show her the guest room, and once she's dropped off her things, we walk through the kitchen and out onto the back porch. The night air is still and warm. The glow of a candle on the wrought iron table lights an open bottle of wine and two glasses, softens the sharp angles of Arthur's profile as he startles up from one of the two chairs.

"Well, um, this is—"

I press a finger against his lips and then kiss him deeply, savoring the taste of red wine and the warmth of his hand as I reach down and squeeze it. When I step back to introduce him to Lily, I lace my fingers into his. "This is Lily. Lily, meet Arthur, my partner. Lily is in a bit of a fix, and I've invited her to spend the night in the guest room."

"Ah, hello, Lily." I make out a hint of confusion, but no hesitation, in Arthur's voice. "Welcome. Would you, um, excuse me while I fetch another chair?"

"Hello, Arthur," Lily says. "Thank you."

I sink into the seat Arthur vacated and motion for Lily to take the other. He comes back out with another chair and a wine glass, sets the chair next to mine, and pours three glasses of wine. Then he raises his glass.

"A more civilized welcome," he says, smiling at Lily. "I hope you like pinot noir."

Arthur and I sip our wine, but Lily sits with one hand on the stem of her glass and the other on her belly. "I do," she says. "But I don't think I should have any. I'm pregnant, you see."

"I should've, um, asked first," Arthur says after a too long moment. "I'm, ah, I'm sorry, Lily."

"It's my fault," I say, feeling as awkward as Arthur sounds. "I ought to have remembered. Can we get you something else?"

"How about a cup of hot apple cider?" Arthur offers.

"That would be nice."

He takes Lily's wine glass and heads back inside.

I wait until the screen door slaps shut behind him, then turn to Lily. "Would it be okay if I shared your story with Arthur? I promise you that it couldn't be in safer or surer hands."

"Is Arthur your husband?"

"Arthur would like that. Very much. But Rooster was the only husband I'll ever have. One was enough."

"But the way you talked about your late husband back at the restaurant," Lily says, "about Rooster I mean, made it seem like—"

"Rooster was the most beautiful man I've ever seen. A hell-for-leather cowboy, and the best dancer I've ever had the pleasure of two-stepping with. We fell in love at a rodeo dance, and he made my life an adventure."

"I don't understand why you wouldn't want that again."

"I don't want love to be an adventure. Life is hard enough as it is. What I want from love is companionship, stability, trust," I raise my wineglass, "and a little romance. The rest is mostly hormones. It took the better part of a lifetime for me to realize that. And I never would've learned it without Arthur."

The screen door swings open, and Arthur bustles back out onto the porch carrying a steaming mug that he sets on the table. The scents of apple and cinnamon fill the night air, and Lily leans her face down into the steam. "It smells wonderful," she says. "Thank you."

Lily sits sipping hot apple cider while Arthur and I drink our wine, and I recount what she said about her search for Augie. "I told you earlier that Lily was in a bit of a fix," I say at last. "I guess I should've said that she's come to a crossroads."

"So you've called and you've texted and you've crisscrossed Texas,"

42

Arthur says. "What now?"

"Now I'm flat broke," Lily says, "and it won't be long before the phone company suspends my account. I'm way past due on the bill. But I'm so close to finding Augie. I know that he's working at one of the construction sites here in Jordan, and tomorrow I'll go around to them all."

"What if I offered you a cashier job at the café, and said that you could stay in the guest room until you get your first paycheck?"

"I'd rather have an old Ford truck and an armload of bluebonnets."

"Fair enough," I say. "But I've got to open up for breakfast at 6 a.m., and it's going on midnight. I told you that I had something I'd like you to see. It's time." I turn to Arthur. "I thought we'd show her the Queen of the Night."

"The queen of the what?" Lily asks.

"Queen of the Night," Arthur chuckles. "It's a cactus. Its proper name is Night-Blooming Cereus. Some people call it *deer-horn*. And for most of the year it looks like a deer horn, or a dead bush. But one night a year, usually around midsummer, it blooms. And the blossoms are the most majestic and fragrant flowers I've ever seen or smelled."

I rest a hand on Arthur's shoulder. "Do you think they've opened up yet?"

"I was out there just before you arrived. There were five or six buds that looked like they were about ready to pop. I'd be willing to bet that we've got some blossoms by now. Shall we go and see?"

The full moon lights the cactus garden in the backyard, the combination stable and hay barn on the far side of the fence, and the open land beyond that stretches away west into the pale distance. Arthur takes my hand and leads me along the stone path that snakes among the cactus beds with Lily walking just behind.

"Watch out for the thorns," Arthur says. "The cacti are beautiful, but they bite."

"Did you plant all of this, May Belle?" Lily asks.

"I'm no gardener. Arthur gave me the plants, and he's the one who tends them. But I do use the peppers that he grows for my chili."

"The Queen of the Night cactus is right over here," Arthur says. "I've trained it to grow up the fence."

In the moonlight I make out the spindly stems of the Queen of the Night that are lead-gray. Speckled like stars against the gray background, I see a half-dozen white flowers. Three of the buds are open—two fully, one

43

partway—and the trumpet-shaped blossoms, waxy and white and many-petaled, smell unbelievably sweet.

"Oh, Arthur," I say, "it's gorgeous."

"Come on up, Lily, and have a look," Arthur says, moving aside to make room. "You can lean in close to get the full impact of the fragrance, but be careful. The stems are covered with spines."

"Okay." Lily steps up next to me, and the two of us press our faces against the open blooms.

"It takes about a half-hour for the flower to fully open once it starts," Arthur says. "It's too slow for you to see. But if you look away for a couple of minutes, and then look back, you'll be able to tell that it's moved."

"And they only last one night?" Lily asks.

"Yes. They'll close forever with the first rays of the sun."

"It seems like such a shame," Lily says, stepping back.

"The flame that burns twice as bright burns half as long." Arthur takes out his pocketknife, cuts the two fully open flowers, hands one each to Lily and me. "You'll be able to see the colors better in the candlelight. You two can stay out here as long as you like, but I'm off to bed."

I brush my lips against Arthur's. "I'll be there in a little while," I whisper. Then I catch his eye and smile in a way that Lily doesn't need to see. Or maybe she does, I realize. Maybe she does at that.

"Thank you for the flower," Lily says. "And for everything."

"Good night," Arthur says, giving me back that same smile.

"Shall we go and have a look at the blossoms in the candlelight?" I ask Lily. Instead of waiting for an answer, I wind my way back through the cactus beds to the porch. Arthur has taken the wine bottle and the glasses, and the only thing left on the table is the candle, blue-flamed at the wick and flickering yellow-orange with each faint breath of the warm night air.

Lily lays her flower next to the candle. I set mine next to Lily's, and we both sit down and study the blooms. The thin, creamy outer petals surround broader pure-white inner petals, which in turn surround bright yellow stamens that protrude in a delicate ring from the center of the blossom. The sweet scent of the flowers wafts up into the air, and in the candlelight I can see that Lily's eyes have filled again with tears.

"This is how I feel inside," she says, nodding down at the flowers, "when I'm with Augie."

"Oh child," I murmur, just loud enough for my words to carry across the table. "Until a minute ago, I had no idea what to say about that feeling. But hear this. There are two kinds of love that I've felt in my life, and two men I've shared that love with. What I had with Rooster was a brushfire, white-hot and fast-moving, and we lived every minute like it was the last one we'd ever get. Arthur and I were good friends before we became lovers. What we have is more like this candle flame: warm and steady, and long-lasting. I'm happier with Arthur."

"And yet you won't marry him."

"He has his house, and I have my house. We spend a lot of time together, but we both have our own spaces when we need to be alone."

"But I don't want to be alone," Lily says.

"Be that as it may, I can tell you for sure that you do have options. I meant what I said earlier about the cashier job and the guest room. Love is more than wildflowers and grand romantic gestures. And your whole life doesn't have to revolve around one man, although it may not seem like that now."

"It doesn't."

"Then I'll tell you one more thing before I turn in," I say. "I have seen Augie. He comes into the Second Chance Café every morning at six for coffee and breakfast tacos." I stand up and take the flower Arthur gave me off the table. "I'll be heading in at 5 a.m. to open up. You're welcome to come with me. What happens after that is up to you."

"What would you do, May Belle?"

I pause at the screen door and look back at Lily as she presses her own cactus flower against her cheekbone. I see the lifepath she'll start down tomorrow blaze out ahead of her: the fiery peaks and the valleys of ashes, the pleasure and the pain, the heartbreak. And nothing that I've said or done tonight will change it. "I'm going to bed," I say. "Goodnight."

"I'll see you in the morning," she says, and the creamy outer petals of the blossom and the paleness of her cheek seem to blend into a single skin.

Asking Oscar about Pal

Dear Oscar, I could start, if I wrote to him, which I would not, though I might write a letter then use it as speaking notes, and *Dear Oscar* sounds good except for the word *dear*, which is way too smulchy for me to use or for Oscar to bear hearing. Just *Oscar*, then: word from the Jasper docs is that my ticker is dangerously close to the two-point-five billion beats allotted to me, and it's pounding its way into the final few hundred thousand. No, Captain Brandan Seymour Blake, that's too frivolous for Oscar, and he could either nod off or refuse my request out of sheer boredom. Start over:

Oscar, I'm dying.

That's too stark, too blunt, and it might get Oscar off on the wrong subject in trying to cheer me up by arguing that I have years left. Years. He would say that. So, Captain Brandan, get to the point, talk about Pal who will need help after I'm dead. *Dear Oscar*. Damn, drop that word.

Oscar, you know about Pal, I could say, how being a parrot he could live to age ninety, something I'll never do. Pal so loves the chinaberry tree that's legally in your yard even if its branches hang into Pal's yard. My yard, I mean. You know how he sits out the warm months in that chinaberry tree, singing to your cats. That's good, appealing to Oscar through his cats.

No, scratch *singing* since everyone knows Pal screeches at the cats, calls them *piss cats* and drags out the ends of those words. "Hey *pissss catssss*." Yeah, like that. But why irritate Oscar about those cats he loves so much? Better to say Pal talks to the cats, and say they understand him, not like you understand your cats. Can't say that–not *your*. Say just *the cats*, since Oscar believes no one can own a cat.

Do I own Pal? I always thought I did, and I've had him thirty years, got him when I was captain of the menhaden boat, fed him fish, too, and he ate menhaden, something I would never do on account of the stink.

No, forget that, Captain, don't talk about fish and stink. You need to come up with something smart and high-minded, something like Grandma did that night she talked Uncle Philip into staying with his wife and working to be a father to her child. Maybe even lead up to talking about the problem of Pal by telling how Grandpa walked with Serena into the woods, blanket under his arm, so he could get a look at her large, um. Can't say *boobs* to Oscar. What, then? *Bosoms*. Then tell of that day, months later, when Uncle Philip returned to Oklahoma after working for nearly a year on the docks in Corpus Christi, home to his parents' house where he had left his cute little wife, home to find Serena large with a child that couldn't be his because of his long absence, and Serena, simple and sweet Serena, pointed to her father-in-law and said right off it was Philip's dad who—

Oscar would like that story, but I need to get to the question about Pal. Get fast to the problem of time and aging and the needs of Pal, the fish-eating parrot who found me thirty years ago, lit on my shoulder right there on the dock beside my menhaden boat with nets hanging all over the deck to dry and smelling of dead fish, lit on this shoulder right here and accused me of being an old fart. First thing out of his beak when we met, him standing on my shoulder, was "Hello, old fart." I figured he was at least ten years old then and knew him to be a male from the blue on the part of the beak around his nose holes, and I named him Pal because you will put up with being hailed as an old fart only by a pal, though for sure he had another name before he flew away from some home in Port Arthur and landed on my shoulder, maybe Polly, a name people hang on parrots, male and female even if Polly should be a girl's name. Maybe they kept him ten years, those Port Arthur folk, likely Cajuns, maybe treated him like an animal instead of a pal, and that made him sulk around for a few years before saying to hell with this crap and flying out of the house and around the city until he spotted the right old fart to take care of him. Animals find you like that. Your cats do that, wander up to you and even if they can't talk like Pal, they manage to say with meows that they have chosen you to take care of them.

So there it is, then. Polly was some ten years old the day he became Pal. That ten plus the thirty he has been with me, many of them in our mutual chinaberry tree singing to your *pissss catssss*. That could leave him another fifty years of life, if the heart beats allotted to a parrot really last ninety years, and I think that number is damn close to the right one. Would Oscar stay awake well enough during the telling of the numbers and the names? He is, after all, close to my age, the age of Charlie, my uncle-cousin, and prone these days to telling me *no* about simple requests. What would he say to a request that's as important to me as his cats are to him, and do I dare mishandle the asking?

Maybe just come out with it and ask Oscar about after my ticker gives out, what becomes of Pal, that wonderful little creature who relies on me to feed him and give him water and keep him warm in the winter and clean the cage he sits in during the night when he cranks up one leg and locks the other and puts his beak in his side feathers so he can sleep? Some say birds put their beaks under their wings to sleep, but Pal never does that. His beak goes close to a wing, but never under it. Every morning he hops right out of that cage, waddles into my bedroom, flies to the foot of my bed and says, "Gimme some bacon, dammit. Bacon. Gimme some bacon." Which he doesn't mean since he's never eaten bacon and he says bacon only because I said it to him enough times that he learned, and he learned if he crabbed at me about bacon every morning, I would get up and give him a morning cookie. He'll eat a cracker because he is after all a parrot, and his previous owners—that is, his previous family—the Cajuns, they no doubt gave him only crackers because that's what people do with parrots they name Polly, give them crackers, but in our home he won't eat a cracker every time you offer one. Sometimes he turns his head to look at the cracker with one eye, then the other before he says, "Gimme some bacon dammit," because he likes cookies a bunch better than crackers.

Maybe I shouldn't say all that about having to feed Pal every morning. It might scare Oscar into refusing to take care of Pal after my last day of heartbeats. Maybe get back to something less demanding, something interesting and safely in the past, like the story of Grandma convincing her son, my uncle Philip, to forgive his cute little wife, though she was far from little that night Philip came home and realized her condition, and she so nervous about it that hours before he arrived and her knowing he would come for sure that day and see her belly, she tried to hang herself.

I could tell Oscar that the hanging was poorly planned, given that Serena stood on a chair beside the rack that held Philip's mother's quilt near the ceiling and out of the way when she and her friends weren't sitting around it to sew all those patches together. Serena took that string dangling from the quilting rack and wound it around her pretty little neck and ...

Sure, Oscar would go for that story, would listen, even lean forward, his lips parted and brows high in astonishment and interest, and that would be good, except that such telling would get me away from the problem of what to do about Pal.

Maybe just say it right off. Oscar, can you find someone to help Pal get food and water after I'm dead? Someone like that little girl who used to live across the street, May Belle, who loved to talk to Pal and laughed every time Pal called the mailman *buzzard breath*, *dung bag*, and *do-do head*? May Belle would love to take care of Pal. But that was years ago, I know, and May Belle is grown and has moved away, and probably has forgotten Pal and his foul mouth, even if she taught him some of those nasty words. Not May Belle then, but someone like her, you know, someone who is only a few hundred million heartbeats into her lifetime, someone whose heart could last long enough for her to help Pal through old age, as I cannot manage no matter how much I wish I could. We make pets dependent on us, something you know, for your cats depend on you, so you and I have a moral obligation to tend to our creatures, to love them, to plan for them when we cannot be around. Okay, not *our* pets, then. I'll say *pets* and leave off the idea of ownership since Oscar believes we don't own our animals.

How could Oscar find such a person as May Belle? Asking that of him might well cause him to balk about helping in any way, make him fear the complexity of looking around Jasper for the right combination of youth and love of birds or maybe just love of animals so he could introduce her to Pal and get her to like him maybe enough to say she would take care of the smart little bird.

I could say, Oscar, do you suppose you could find a girl who—but hey. Why a girl? Why not a boy? But maybe it would be best not to bring up that problem along with all the others, though I could, of course—yeah, and then Oscar might get bored and his attention drift off with my having so many angles to explain and suggest. I've seen him nodding off right there in front of me, best friend or not, for he once told me I can be a tedious old fart in telling so many stories. A wise plan would be to have a good tale up my sleeve for when his eyes start to glaze over with all the fiddle-faddle about finding a younger May Belle to take care of Pal. I need to hold his attention.

This would serve my purpose: Oscar, did I ever tell you about the time my aunt Serena tried to hang herself?

It didn't work out exactly the way she thought it might, if she ever did any such thinking. When she jumped off that chair, the string jerked the whole quilting rack off the ceiling with such a racket that Grandpa and Grandma both came running and found Serena all bruised and with a string burn on her neck. Grandma told me years later that Grandpa spent the day looking hang-dog sorry for his part in the family shame so obvious in Serena's big belly, and Grandma spent many hours that day crying and coming up with a plan for what to say to my uncle Philip after he took a look at Serena.

Oscar, I could tell him, Grandma soothed Philip that night in the big family pow-wow around the dinner table, told him that the child in

50

Serena's belly was his flesh-and-blood brother or sister even if the child was not his own son or daughter, and that he had the moral obligation to take care of the child. Philip said it was his father's seed and thus his obligation, but his mama pointed out that Philip's father was old and in weak health and wouldn't last long enough to see the child get through school much less get married, that time was for sure against any solution except Philip's taking the baby on as his very own child, for it was Serena's and she was his wife, so by any moral measure that baby was his, too.

Maybe go on to tell Oscar that it turned out to be a boy, one Philip and Serena named Charlie, a boring little kid I didn't like much, he being actually my age and a relentless talker as a little kid, then a braggart as a teenager, and a story-topper. In his twenties a real bore. In his forties and fifties and on to now in his seventies, Charlie has a way of leaning into your space while he talks, backing you all around the room and never noticing that you step back when he moves toward you, he being so intent on the telling that little bits of white foam build up in the corners of his ever-moving mouth, and he holds his eyes wide open for emphasis so you can see the whites of his eyes all around the green-yellow orbs in the center. I can tell Oscar how I took to calling him Chum Lee, slurring the words, making them sound a little like Charlie and all the while wanting to render him into real chum and pour the goop of his body into the ocean to attract fish. Not that I ever would kill him or wish him to die, just that I wanted him to shut up, especially when he got wound up about something he knew absolutely nothing about, like the time he told me all birds could learn to talk just like parrots if you took a sharp knife and split their little tongues, then spent the time necessary to teach them some words. Sparrows even? I asked, with their tiny little brains and stupid one-note chirps? And he said "yes," his eyelids going up too high while he moved into my space so I had to step back. Then, he added that sparrows are moral little things and so simple they can learn only about a dozen words, and they refuse to learn nasty words, and I said, "Wow, Chum Lee, that's amazing!" while I wasn't amazed at all but was thinking about his being turned into fish chum and dumped into the sea.

Did you know, Oscar, I could say at this point, there is a company that makes Menhaden Milk? No kidding, that's what they call it. Menhaden Milk. They make it from the very fish, menhaden, that I used to catch out in the Gulf. I caught them by the thousands, and they were not good for anything except to make dog food stink of fish, though Pal would nibble on one every time we dragged up the nets to dip the menhaden into the hold of the ship. Back then, some people used menhaden as chum to attract fish for line fishermen. But would Oscar give a damn about bottled Menhaden Milk sold for chum or that to this day, after all these years and Charlie's heart like mine approaching two-and-a-half-billion beats, I still call him Chum Lee and have never told him that our grandfather was actually his father and that Charlie is my uncle, not my cousin?

The cat man would listen, all right, because the story is so weird, but would he really care about the people in my story enough to hear me out, to still be alert when I got to the part about Pal and the ticking away of time?

My buddy Oscar, who listens to cats and dreams that they talk to him without words, teaching him to be present, always to live in the present, or so he claims, might not give a damn about Menhaden Milk or Chum Lee or about the crash of that quilting rack way back in the last century before I was born, before Pal was hatched, even. Oscar might listen for only so long before nodding off during the telling, so Pal will wind up without a caretaker after my two-point-five-billion heartbeats are over. Still, I must try, for Pal's sake, for my sake.

Dear Oscar—ah, that *dear* again, the wrong word. I need to say in writing to Oscar, let's talk about Charlie calling me cousin when we're not cousins at all, to say let's talk about my grandfather walking into the woods with a blanket under his arm and holding hands with my aunt Serena, about Pal and the chinaberry tree and May Belle teaching him to say *do-do head*, about cats and the stink of menhaden, and most about how time these days runs lean as a tired clock winding down, so we need to do something about Pal.

Levee Cutters

"Stay out of sight. One of those Cajuns might see us and try to pick us off with a rifle." Lugar gestured toward the new housing development. He and Rey hunkered down on the marsh side of the levee.

As Rey watched with astonishment, Lugar pulled a gold necklace from a pocket, brought it to his lips, then flung it into the bayou.

"You threw away gold," Rey said. "Gold."

"I bought it for that two-timing bitch. Fifty-timing. A hundred, for all I know. I drowned more than gold."

"Why didn't you bury it with the engagement ring?"

"Only the ring belonged in that grave."

It was a ceremony that Rey had not understood, Lugar taking him to the edge of Hildebrandt Bayou, handing him a shovel, asking for help with the digging. Lugar took a lingering look at the ring, snapped the box closed, and set it in the ground like a coffin.

"That ring is worth some big bucks," Rey said. "And you're throwing it away?"

"This is a burial of the dead, not just a ring," Lugar had said.

So Rey knew asking about the drowning of the necklace would get him no answers that made sense. "Okay, then. Tell me how we're going to chop this levee."

"We make a narrow cut with the barbed wire, you on one side of the levee, me on the other, using the wire like a two-man saw. When high water comes, it'll worm into the cut, and before you know it, the levee gives way. But I need to know why you're willing to flood out all those houses."

"I told you already."

"To save crabs and guppies. That sounds too goofy even for a good reason, much less a real one."

"And your reason isn't goofy? To punish Celestine, hah." Rey felt inclined to say more, but he was a bit afraid of angering Lugar.

"What I mean is," Lugar said, "I brought barbed wire and heavy gloves. But we should understand why you're letting in the flood waters. A passel of crabs don't seem to count for much."

The wind picked up and brought with it the smell of the Gulf. Salt water, Rey thought. Seaweed. He took a deep breath to savor the aroma as it blended with the living smells of sawgrass and bayou. "High tide's on the way, not to mention all the rain coming with the hurricane. We better do the cutting."

"I've got reason enough. You?"

"Not just crabs." Rey waved a hand toward the marshlands. "The whole place is teeming with life. Deer, osprey, armadillo, to name a few. Rabbits, crabs—blue, flat backs, fiddler—a dozen kinds, all a part of the living marshland. This place is home to turtles beautiful enough to make you cry, alligators ugly enough to deserve to live, great blue heron, lesser blues, red-wings, not to mention nutria rats."

"Every one of those animals can run, swim or fly, and they're survivors, animals who like the marsh."

"Hurricane high water kills enough to knock a hole even in this teeming mass of life. The flood will destroy their breeding grounds unless we let the water drain some by cutting the levee."

"What if the water we let in drowns some of the Cajuns, drowns them right in their houses? You saying you care more for gators and pollywogs than you care for people?"

"Maybe." Rey pretended to consider the matter, tried for a brow wrinkled in heavy and important thought, then realized the deepening twilight hid his efforts from Lugar. "The only Cajun you care about is Celestine LeBlanc. You would never try to drown her."

"Care about her? Hell no. I hate her. Did you know the cat round-up man, what's-his-name, Cecil, did her in his pickup? Parked right there in front of her house."

The anger in Lugar's voice made Rey plenty nervous. For weeks Lugar had called Celestine an angel and a beauty queen and the only woman for him, sentiments that made Rey even more jumpy after the night Celestine took him from a Procter Street nightclub to a hotel, she in a heated rush of musk, laughter, and demands. In the morning, more sober, Rey told her he couldn't see her again, that he was ashamed for doing Lugar's woman. But he wasn't ashamed so much as worried about what his friend would do if he found out.

There were plenty other guys Celestine had her way with, or so Rey had heard. Then on the very day Lugar had intended to give Celestine the engagement ring, he found her and Cecil Jubak going at it in a pickup.

"So you want to drown Celestine," Rey said.

"Hell no. I just want to make her suffer, same as she did me, same as I did to get back at Al Boudreau. Did I ever tell you about the jumbo shrimp I hid in his car?"

Rey had heard the story before, but he knew that, whatever his answer, he was about to hear it again, so he said, "No. Tell me about the shrimp."

"I pulled the hubcaps off his car, put three gigantic shrimp in each, and popped caps back on. Took me less that five minutes, but it took Al weeks of scrubbing out his car, trying to cure the stink. He took the seats out, peeled off the upholstery, burned candles in the car, squirted all sorts of perfumes, and none of it did any good. Months after the smell finally wore off, he found the shrimp hulls while changing a flat, so he knew someone did a number on him. Trouble was, he didn't know who did it because he had so many enemies that it could have been any of fifty. Hundred. More, maybe."

"Cutting the levee," Rey said, "is a shrimp-in-the-hubcap slap at Celestine, then."

"Yeah. Same as. It will take her weeks, maybe months to get the wet and the mold out of her house. While she does all that work, you know what I'll be? Glad. Yeah. Glad. Her suffering is a good reason and a real reason all wrapped into one. You have a good reason, all them critters you're boo-hooing about. But you got to have a real reason, and I need to know it."

"I want to discourage builders from taking over the marsh for houses, to show it's dangerous to build in tidewater land, even with levees. Soon the whole marshland from Port Arthur to Winnie will be crusted over with roads, so you could roller skate in any direction. Then goodbye to the wildlife."

Lugar nodded. "That works for me, though I figured you was also after punishing Celestine, like maybe you was one of the fifty guys who diddled her. A hundred. It's a relief to me that you had nothing to do with her."

Rey felt his throat go dry. "I hope—"

"No need to talk now." Lugar said. "Put on these leather gloves and help me unroll the barbed wire."

II. Living in the Moment and Other Philosophies

Flight

I wade into the yowling, fur-covered swarm that converges on my boots as I approach the food pans. I stumble, manage to recover, stumble again. Then, resisting the urge to kick cats in all directions—as I've seen my father do, sending felines flying end-over-end like point-after-tries into the yard—I grab the door handle, swing the back door gently into the swirling black-and-white-and-orange mass, squeeze through the narrow space between the handle and jamb, and slip cat-free into the house.

The aroma of bacon and eggs and biscuits still saturates the inside air.

"Cat bait," my father called the breakfast smell, black-dark early, when we sat down to eat at 5:30 and the first plaintive meows began on the back porch. By the time my mother served steaming cups of black coffee, the caterwauling had reached a fever pitch. The old man winced, shook his head at the sound, met my eyes across the table. "Chum," he said, nodding down at the bright yellow platter between us piled high with breakfast food. He shook his head again, this time at me. "Are you and Cecil sure y'all want to do this cat-fishing thing?"

"Yes sir." I raised my coffee cautiously, blowing steam from its surface. "Cecil's bringing a casting net. Says he's been practicing. He's supposed to be here at 6:30, and I've got a bundle of towsacks already stacked on the carport."

"Fair enough. But I don't want your mother to've made all this extra food for nothing. And I won't put up with that plague of porch cats even one more day. Get it done with the casting net this morning, or I'll handle it myself with the shotgun this afternoon."

I gulped coffee, the searing liquid caught in the back of my throat and burned, and for an eternal moment—as I pictured my father blasting cats with a double-barrel twelve-gauge—it was all I could do not to spray a scalding mix of coffee and spit into the old man's face. The cats were feral, having wandered up onto the back porch over the course of the hardest winter to hit Southwest Texas in forty years. They ate up the dry food and scraps that were supposed to feed the dogs; they dug into the trash cans; and worse, they crawled up into warm truck engines on frigid nights and got shredded by radiator fans in the early morning dark—with a sickening *whump-whump-whump*—damaging engine parts and upsetting my mother. And me. I understood that the cats needed to go. I just didn't have it in me to do it the old man's way.

But I knew better than to say so. Instead I choked down the last of my scrambled eggs, got up from the table, and headed outside to haul the dogs down to the hay barn and chain them.

Back in the dining room now, with the mantel clock over the corner fireplace showing 6:25, I have five minutes left before Cecil arrives with the net. Just enough time for a test run. The platter of leftover bacon and eggs and biscuits still sits on the table, but the rest of the breakfast mess has been cleared away. I make out, over the back-porch caterwauling, the soothing sound of dishes clinking together in the kitchen sink.

Then the dishwashing suddenly stops. "Joey?" my mother calls.

"Yes ma'am?"

"Have you figured out what you're going to tell Cecil about college?"

I slump against the door. It seems like the shotgun ultimatum ought to be enough for one morning. I'm still sweating from the effort of chaining up four big dogs that didn't want to be chained, and the t-shirt clings to my back where it presses against the wood. "Does it have to be today?"

"You promised me, son. If I fixed all that extra food this morning, you said you'd show Cecil those letters and tell him about your change in plans." She pauses, and I can almost see her standing there at the sink with a soapy sponge in one hand and a greasy plate in the other, worry lines creased into her forehead and around her eyes. Waiting for me to do the right thing. "We're into March now, Joey. It's time."

"It's past time," I say finally, knowing she's right but dreading what's coming. "I'll get it done."

I walk to my bedroom, fetch the two envelopes off my dresser, set them on the table next to the bait. Both are addressed to *Joseph Jasmine, Jr.* One has a Colorado Springs, Colorado postmark. The other is from Austin. As I scoop a spoonful from the mound on the platter and wade back out into the yowling swarm to make my test run, the eggs and bacon and biscuits I ate earlier harden like cement in my guilt-heavy belly.

I sling the food into the nearest pan and feel my boots suddenly free of cat pressure when the entire throng converges on the decoy, as expected. I nod, walk to the edge of the porch, stare up into the sky. The stars are fading, the Southwest Texas hills backlit by the coming day. In the first red rays of the rising sun, the Indian paintbrushes that dot the pasture look like drops of blood floating on a pool of deep green coastal Bermuda, and the prickly pear in the fenceline is covered with crimson blooms. But

I'm thinking about Cecil, and about the letters. The one from Colorado, dated a week ago, is an offer from the Air Force Academy to train me as a pilot—something Cecil and I have dreamed of since we were four years old, sitting in front of the TV in my living room and watching the first man walk on the moon. At thirteen in the big sycamore out front that served as our rocket ship, we recited "High Flight," the sonnet all fourth-class cadets have to declaim from memory, and swore a blood oath to attend the Academy together to become fighter pilots and then astronauts. The other letter, dated February 15th, is a scholarship offer to study classical languages and cultures at the University of Texas. And despite my oath to soar with Cecil up the long, delirious, burning blue and touch the face of God, I yearn with my whole heart to go to Austin.

The *chunk* of a shovel biting into soft ground snaps my attention back down to earth. A little way up the fence line, Moisés Mercado—a Mexican national who has worked every March through December for my father since before I was born—is digging up a fencepost that the bulls snapped in two yesterday. Once the broken-off piece is out of the ground, Moisés and I will set the new post together and retighten the strands of barbed wire.

"It's early to be out digging," I call, loud enough to cover the twenty yards between the porch and the broken post.

Moisés shakes his head and grins. "*¡En español!*"

"*No hay problema,*" I say, smiling back. This is a game the two of us have played since I turned ten and was put to work before school and after, on weekends, and through the grueling summers with their searing heat and blowing dust. "*Es pronto para estar fuera de excavación,*" I say again. During my eight years of working with Moisés, I've learned to speak Spanish like a native; and for the past two years, my Spanish teacher at Jordan High School has taught me formal grammar. The words come so easily, the way things do when you really love them. And that love has supplanted my boyhood desire to soar away into blue.

"I didn't come early for the digging," Moisés says. "I came for the show."

"*¿El espectáculo?*" I repeat. We're both speaking Spanish now. "I don't understand."

"The cat rodeo," Moisés says. "Your father told me about the tow sacks, and about the net." The grin splits his sun-leathered face like the post he's excavating. "I wouldn't miss it. Not for all the tequila in Jalisco."

61

I feel my own smile fade. It's obvious now what my father thinks about the chances of getting rid of the cats my way. And Moisés clearly shares the old man's opinion. More determined than ever that the twelve-gauge will stay in the gun cabinet, I turn my back on Moisés and head for the carport.

I pause to make a rough estimate of cat numbers as I skirt the porch. About three dozen, I guess. Clumped around the food pans, growling and hissing and tussling over scraps, the cats are impossible to really count. And Cecil is overdue. But the carport, which we plan to use as a staging area, is ready to go. I moved my mother's Suburban to the edge of the backyard last night, and left my own beat-up old ranch truck down at the hay barn. My father took off in the four-wheel drive a half-hour ago to check the cattle.

I cross the covered concrete slab, strap on my work gloves, and start counting out tow sacks. The bundle sits next to the faded red roping dummy that the old man used to teach me to lasso cattle off a horse. I drape each brown burlap bag over the welded-pipe horns as I count, remembering the acrid smell of Grullo, my big gray roan, sweating underneath me in the summer sun and the mind-numbing repetition—heading, heeling, heading, heeling—with the dummy steer swinging around on its pivot each time I managed to drop my loop over the horns, and my father effortlessly catching the welded-pipe heels with every toss. As much as I love Grullo and the rest of the horses, I've always hated cattle—hulking, stupid, shit-smelling, walking hamburgers—even more. And the fall and spring roundups are the bane of my existence, the things I most look forward to leaving behind when this senior year is finally done. Despite the Spanish lessons, patching barbed wire fences isn't a whole lot better.

Two more months, and I'm gone.

Just as that thought flashes through my mind, I make out a low rumble from the direction of the highway. Cecil. Has to be. As I count out my twentieth tow sack, the rumble becomes a roar. I look up to see Cecil's bright red truck shoot past the big sycamore that was our rocket ship, and the site of our blood oath, and feel the breakfast harden again in my belly. But the time for talk about the future is later, after the cats have been caught and delivered, and Cecil has a little cash in his hands. In the meantime I square my shoulders, scoop up the tow sacks, and walk out to meet the best friend I plan to betray.

"Is everything ready to go?" Cecil asks, hopping out of the truck almost before it stops moving. "What do the numbers look like?" The dust cloud of his passing sweeps across the two of us as he heads straight for the back porch.

No pause for a greeting, I think to myself. No apology for being late. But under the circumstances, I decide to let it pass. "Thirty-six, more or less."

Cecil stops abruptly, swinging around to face me. "What do you mean *more or less*?"

"I mean if you think you can do a better job of counting that cat swarm," I say, "have at it."

"Mmm ..." He slits his eyes in the direction of the back porch and works his tongue around in his mouth as if taste-testing the possibilities. He calls it *savoring the angles*, and there is nobody better at it than Cecil. In the same way that I've always been book-smart, Cecil is business-smart. It seems like, no matter what the payoff, he can figure a way to get a taste of the pie. The money end of the cat operation was entirely his idea. "No," he says at last. "Like I told you before, Rooster Stiles says he'll only pay us for twenty. Five dollars a cat—adults only, no kittens—a hundred dollars max. We'll just count 'em as we catch 'em. Unless you think your pop might sweeten the pot with a little bonus money. Say a dollar a head?"

"Not a chance," I say, remembering the shotgun ultimatum but keeping it to myself. "The old man says he wants to hold on to a dozen or so anyway, to keep the rat numbers down and the rattlesnakes away from the house."

"Yep. That's what Rooster's paying us for. Says his barn's so full of rats they're fouling the hay. Says the horses won't eat it." He glances down at my boots. "Speaking of horses, what you got that shit-kicker regalia on for? This is a cat-fishing operation, not a rodeo."

I give one of Cecil's white leather sneakers a quarter-strength kick with a worn brown boot. "First pile of cat crap you step in will answer that," I say. "And speaking of cat-fishing, where's the net?"

"Almost forgot." He trots back to the truck and returns with an armload of white mesh. A rope is attached to a swivel threaded onto what looks like an open cone at the top end of the netting; on the bottom end, a heavy line weighted with sinkers has been sewn around the perimeter. "Feast your eyes," he says.

"Are you sure you know how to use that thing?"

"I practiced after school yesterday until it was too dark to see. Got me out of mucking stalls. Under the circumstances, Pop's all about me making as much extra money as I can."

"What circumstances?" I ask, my gut a conglomerate rock of guilt and suspicion. Cecil's mother and mine get together for coffee and gossip at least three days a week. But surely she wouldn't have said anything about the letters yet. "Is there something I should know?"

"No time right now. Later maybe. I told Rooster we'd deliver the cats at eight, and it's pushing seven."

"An hour?" I eye the net doubtfully. "We're only going to get one chance at this. Don't you think you'd better take a warm-up throw?"

"Don't need one." Cecil slides his right hand through a loop at the end of the top-rope. "This is the hand line," he says. He coils the rope around his right forearm, then firmly grasps the weighted line around the bottom of the net with his left hand. "This is the lead line. I toss and spread the net with my left hand. I guide and set the net with my right. See?" He makes a mock throw, keeping hold of the net. "You just bunch those cats up tight. I'll cast this thing over 'em sure as sunup."

"We'll need to anchor the net down once the cats are underneath it. Give me a minute." I put the tow sacks down on the back porch next to the trash cans, then I take a dozen white bricks from the big stack left over from building the house and set them next to the sacks. "Now come on," I say. "Slow and easy."

Cecil sidles up next to me, and the two of us survey the cat situation. It looks as though someone has spread a blanket of black and white and orange fur outside the back door. Cats of all colors cover the porch, basking in the light of the sun that has cleared the low hills now and is warming the cement.

"Gravy," he says, licking his lips. Then he raises the net, partially spreading the bottom with this left hand. "You ready to make some easy money?"

"As soon as the scraps hit the pans," I say, "those cats will be all over them. Don't wait for me to get clear. Go ahead and cast the net. I'll be out of the way by the time it gets there. Okay?"

"Okay." Cecil juts his chin in the direction of the fence line. "But what the hell is he doing?"

On the far side of the pasture fence, Moisés leans on his shovel and stares at Cecil and me. The grin still splits his face like the post he's supposed to be digging out.

"*Está mirando el espectáculo,*" I say.

"Say what?"

"Watching the show," I say impatiently, this time in English. Although Cecil has taken the same two years of Spanish as me, he's gotten through mostly by copying my homework and crib-noting the tests. "Let's go."

I ease back around to the carport and slip into the house, hoping to avoid my mother. Through the kitchen and into the dining room, I see no sign of her. But the letters have been pulled from their envelopes and left lying open on the table next to the breakfast scraps. A reminder, I realize. And a threat. If I don't tell Cecil about my decision to break our blood oath, she'll do it herself. Slowly, as I stare down at the open letters—my letters, my future, my choice—I feel the rock in my belly melt in a frustration-fueled fire that fills my whole body like the scalding coffee I choked on at the old man's shotgun ultimatum. I'm furious at my father, at my mother, at my best friend, even at the cats—so absolutely livid at being trapped in the middle of all their needs and expectations that my fingers shake as I snatch up the cat bait and let the letters lie.

I swing open the back door, toss the entire plate of bacon and eggs and biscuits into the nearest pan, and feel my hemmed-in world grind down into slow motion. Feral cats swarm the food pan. The casting net swirls out of Cecil's hands and spreads like a sail. I plant a boot, leap over the cats, duck under the net, swing my body around in midair, and land hard on my hands and knees in the grass between two piles of cat crap.

The casting net settles gently over the tight-packed black-and-white-and-orange mass engaged in its feeding frenzy. And for a long moment, all is still. I glance away at the fenceline and see, instead of a grin, a mix of shock and amazement on Moisés's face. I glance over at Cecil, and the look on his face is the same. Even the cats seem awestruck, crouching silently under the nylon mesh.

In the next instant, fueled by the anger that still bubbles inside me, I swing into action. I run to the trash cans, grab an armload of rough white bricks, and set each one just inside the weighted line at the perimeter of the net. I make another trip, and another. Moisés and Cecil never move. But in a matter of seconds all twelve bricks are in place, and the cats—which suddenly begin flopping and floundering and fighting the nylon mesh—are securely held.

"I did it!" Cecil crows, slipping the hand line from around his wrist. "Didn't I tell you I'd do it? Gravy. Didn't I say so?"

I have to grind my teeth together to keep from saying something I know I'll regret.

"Now all we have to do is stuff the cats into tow sacks." Cecil fetches the sacks I counted out and shakes the first one open. "Twenty of them anyway. I'll hold the bags, you stuff the cats. Then we'll deliver them to Rooster and collect our pay."

"That's a bad idea," I hear. In Spanish. From the fence line. And despite the liquid heat of the wrath threatening to spill out of me, I look over to see Moisés shaking his head in the direction of the porch. "A very bad idea. Don't do it."

"What the hell is his problem?" Cecil asks, shaking the tow sack.

Instead of answering, I reach under the net, grab a cat by the scruff of the neck, and haul it out. The cat, a black-and-white-and-orange calico with a two-inch stump for a tail—the rest having been hacked off by an engine fan—arches its back, spreads its legs wide, and bares its claws as I swing it toward the open sack. The back claws catch the burlap, allowing the animal to spin in a whirlwind of fangs and talons. And with a spitting snarl, the calico shreds my arms that are bare above my work gloves, then shoots across the yard leaving a bloody trail of bites and scratches from my wrists to my armpits.

"I told you that was a bad idea," I hear in Spanish from the fence line. "I wouldn't try it again."

"What did he say?" Cecil asks, glancing from the blood on my arms to the cats floundering under the net.

"He said it's your turn to try cat-stuffing," I say through clenched teeth.

"He did not. And anyway, what the hell would a wetback know about stuffing cats into tow sacks?"

"Moisés is not a wetback," I hiss. "Now gimme that bag."

"Then gimme those gloves."

We trade out, and I shake open the tow sack while Cecil reaches under the net, grabs a cat by the scruff of the neck, and hauls it out. This time the cat is a coal-black tom with its tail intact. But the result is the same—a blur of claws and fangs and blood in fast motion—the only difference being that it's Cecil left staring down at his shredded arms while the cat shoots across the yard.

"So much for what Moses knows," Cecil says. "Oh, excuse me: *Moisés*. And unless you figure that son of a bitch parted the Rio Grande and walked across the dry riverbed, he's a wetback all right."

I feel my wrath bubbling toward rage. But the pain in my arms perfectly balances the white heat that fills the rest of me, and with a supreme effort of will, I manage to ignore Cecil. "What would you do?" I ask Moisés in Spanish.

"Put the cats into those metal trash cans instead of into the tow sacks," Moisés says. "They can't dig their claws in that way. They'll go right in."

"Goddamnit!" Cecil throws the work gloves at me. "Stop talking gobbledygook with that wetback and grab another cat. We've got a deadline to meet."

My first punch, a looping roundhouse, glances off the side of Cecil's head. But the second, an uppercut, catches him square on the jaw. He goes down, and I leap on top of him, and we roll over and over across the porch. He scrambles on top, and I feel a solid punch connect with my left cheek. And another. Then I feel him wrap both hands around my throat and squeeze. Until finally, I manage to roll on top again and pin his arms against his sides.

"I'm not going to the Air Force Academy!" I yell into Cecil's fight-reddened face. "I'm not training to be a pilot! I'm going to the University of Texas to study Latin instead!"

He blinks, bug-eyed. "You mean you actually got into the Academy?"

"Hell yes. Didn't you?"

"Sons of bitches turned me down. I got the rejection letter last Saturday, and I've been trying to figure out how to tell you ever since."

It's my turn to blink, bug-eyed. "I got the acceptance letter last Saturday. And I've been trying ... Damn. I'm sorry I hit you, Cecil."

"Yeah, yeah. Now get the hell off me. I'm laying in cat shit, and you're bleeding on my shirt."

"I always figured we'd both get accepted." I get to my feet and help Cecil up. "I've spent the last week eating my heart out because of our blood oath."

"Truth be told, I don't much care. I don't really want to go to college at all. What I'd like to do is go into business for myself."

"You mean take over your old man's ranch?"

"Hell no. I'm out of here. There's no future in middle-of-nowhere Southwest Texas." Cecil looks me square in the eye. "Are you serious about going to Austin?"

"I've never been more serious about anything in my life."

"Then I'm sorry I choked you."

"So we're both sorry," I say. "What now?"

He slits his eyes and works his tongue around in his mouth. "I've got a business proposition for you," he says slowly. "Hear me out. There's a construction boom going on in Austin right now. Apartments, condos, you name it and they're building it. I was thinking about moving up there and starting my own subcontracting company. My uncle L.B. has got some connections. There'll be work for us both."

"You mean we'd be partners?"

"Not exactly. I was offering you a job. But we could rent an apartment together," he says. "Be roommates."

"Even with the scholarship they're offering, I can't afford to live in the dorms."

"Then I'd like to propose a new oath," Cecil says. "Instead of flight school, we go to Austin together. We get the hell out of Southwest Texas the day after graduation, and we never look back." He holds out his right forearm that is still oozing blood. "What do you say?"

I extend my own still-bleeding forearm and press it against Cecil's. "Done," I say. Then I shake his hand.

"Now we've got some cats to deliver," he says. "Does your buddy down at the fenceline have a better idea than the tow sacks?"

"Moisés says we should stuff the cats into the metal trash cans instead. Says they can't use their claws that way."

Cecil looks ruefully at the shredded skin on his arms. "Sounds good to me."

An hour later, we're sliding the last of four trash cans into the bed of Cecil's truck. Except for the rotten meat smell from the trash bags we had to pull out of the cans to make room for the cats, it was almost fun.

"Better late than never," Cecil says. "Let's go get paid."

"You go ahead. All that's left is to turn the cats loose in Rooster's barn. And I've got work to do here." I nod at Moisés, who has gone back to digging.

"What about the money?"

"You can have my half. You've got a business to start in Austin, and I'm counting on you for a job."

As Cecil roars away in a cloud of dust, I walk to the back porch and gather up the casting net, sending the remaining cats scattering in all directions. Then I grab a shovel from the tool shed and head down to help patch the fence. The sun is climbing higher in the sky, the heat already starting to build. But I find myself smiling. "Dos meses más," I say, savoring the words as Moisés and I lift out the broken post together. Two more months.

Cat Man and the Mystic

"You release them cats again on my property, and I'll sure as hell shoot you." Jesse's voice was tight with anger.

"Yeah," Cecil said. "Right. You'll kill me over some feral cats."

"Didn't say kill. Said shoot. In the leg, maybe, to make you hop around worse than any three-legged dog. Or shoot you in the butt. And don't think for a minute I won't. We had a deal, remember?"

The old man watching the exchange stood by a pecan tree in Jesse's backyard. He held a calico cat, stroked its fur. "Bad plan, Jesse," the old man said.

"I'll deal with that silly threat later," Cecil told the old man. "First problem is to catch the cats again, and that won't be easy."

"Bird shot will knock off some of your hide," Jesse said. "Right off your butt or whatever I happen to hit when I shoot."

"So much for my thinking I was nearly a member of your family, Jesse," Cecil said.

Joe Jasmine, his roommate in Austin, had recommended Cecil for the job. "Uncle Jesse has a cat problem, and you are just the person to help," Joe said. "You and your nets. My uncle will pay you well. But watch out for Jesse's crazy old father-in-law. He is as nutty as a pecan orchard in the fall, and he's the one who keeps all those cats around, somewhere between one and two hundred of them."

Cecil opened the door of his pickup, determined to head for the woods near the boat launch on the Angelina. Bevilport, the locals called it, though there was no town. It was the place he had released the cats. "Damn this work anyway," he mumbled, for he had thought he was finished with Jesse's cat job. He felt inclined to swear with some truly nasty words, loud this time, for he knew that catching even a small percent of the cats would be both hard work and unlikely. A glance at the old man was enough to choke back the swearing.

"I'll go with you," the old man offered, and Cecil nodded.

He had caught the cats, twenty-four of them, with a net of his own design, which he called his dip net. It was large, one that resembled the butterfly nets he had used as a child but much more substantial. On his first job as a cat man and working with his buddy Joe, he had used a fisherman's cast net. That net worked well enough, but he improved the catching with the dip net, and he raised his fee for ridding customers of unwanted cats.

After catching a few more cats than the number Jesse had specified and distributing them among the six thirty-gallon trash cans he kept in the back of his truck, Cecil had driven to the Angelina River, parked in an isolated part of the woods, and released the cats.

With a heavy sigh and a stab of guilt, Cecil watched Oscar Carlson get into the pickup. The old man still held a calico cat. "I can do this," Cecil muttered, keeping the words low so the old boy wouldn't hear. "I can do this."

The calico looked at him and flattened its ears.

Oscar told himself again that he rather liked this boy Cecil, especially since he agreed to try returning the cats he stole. "This lady is Kittykens Eighteen," Oscar said. "She's a tortoise-shell calico."

"You introduced us already." Cecil started the truck, backed down the driveway beside Jesse's two-story house.

"All cats with three colors are female. All of them. Males have one color and at most two."

"You told me that, too."

"I know. I forget. She's a favorite even if I shouldn't have favorites among the tribe of kittykens. But this girl is a sweetheart. Never bites or scratches me. Isn't afraid of anything, even riding in cars. Or trucks. And she always has things to teach me."

Oscar could feel the rumble of the cat's purring, and he regarded the purr as a gift for its bringing him more completely into the present moment. That, Oscar knew, is where cats live: in the eternal present. Oscar repeated the words to himself:

In the eternal present, in the eternal present.

He let the phrase run its linear way inside his head, using the words as a mantra. In a distracting moment of pleasure, he remembered trying to tell Cecil about the wisdom of cats, and the boy seemed on the verge of understanding.

Monkey mind, he chided for leaking himself into the past, for conjuring such memories, and he looked at the trees as the pickup took him toward the river. Pine, magnolia, oak, pecan, sweetgum—monkey mind again, Oscar told himself before slipping back into the beauty of the leaves and pine needles—let the trees join, yes, into this dance of green, this celebration of leaf, blossom, and bole, the clouds beyond them, the ponds spinning by, the purring eternal calico, hands on its fur, the sun breaking through a cloud, all chiming in universal harmony.

The moment gripped Oscar with the rumble of the truck engine, of the feline purr, of the voice from Cecil saying something, and that voice turning green in blending with the forever dance of trees, wind, ponds, clouds—and that spot of sun so tiny becoming smaller yet filling all vision until there was nothing except the light, the light. And in that light, Oscar understood. Everything.

When the swirl of light, sound, and leaf separated into fragments again, Oscar stroked the cat and made himself look at Cecil, forced himself to listen to the words that were no longer a green rumble of harmony, and he felt grief for the passing of blending, wished for another small forever to drift into, but he knew his monkey mind would not allow it, perhaps for a long time. Years, maybe, for this experience was the first in—how long? Ah, he waved a hand in disgust with himself for again misunderstanding time. Kittykens Eighteen looked at him, her eyes showing surprise. Yet, he conceded, there is still a glow of forever around me, and as Cecil spoke words, Oscar could in this new and fallen moment assemble the words into such a meaning as could be found in the ordinary.

"Oscar?" Cecil shifted uneasily in the truck seat and wondered if the old man was having a stroke or maybe a TIA. "You okay, Oscar?"

"Yes. Better. And I feel more like I do now than I have in years, for in this truck and with this cat, I learned something important. I would explain it to you if it could be put into words."

Such an odd thing to say, Cecil thought. The previous day, Jesse had warned that Oscar was unbalanced and prone to say goofy things. "A lunatic of an old man, my father-in-law," Jesse said. "Keeps a jillion feral cats with them breeding like rabbits, and he names every damned one of them the same Swedish sounding name, kittykens, and he uses a number as a last name. How that crazy old guy can tell the difference between Kittykens Seventy-Eight and Kittykens Seventy-Nine is a mystery to me."

Cecil had heard other tales about Oscar Carlson, mostly from his roommate Joe Jasmine. "There's not much traffic on Verna Street in Jasper," Joe once told him. "But what there is could well kill the old boy. He has a habit of entertaining himself by standing on the edge of the street and reading license plates of passing cars. Someday a driver might run over the old bugger."

"Why in the world would he read license plates?" Cecil asked.

"Uncle Jesse thinks he entertains himself by playing some sort of game in his head, something really weird like maybe adding the numbers on the plates and calculating the square root of the sum of those numbers."

"No," Cecil said. "Nobody is that smart or that bizarre."

"Oscar is. So watch him carefully when you deal with all his cats."

The more Cecil talked to Oscar Carlson, the more it seemed clear that the old man was smart enough to do in his head whatever the hell he wanted to do with numbers. And he was as odd as he was smart. Maybe more weird than smart.

As he turned on the dirt road beside the boat launch, Cecil glanced uneasily at Oscar and his calico. The cat looked back with eyes slanted into distrust and with flattened and twitching ears. Oscar had his eyes closed and had an inscrutable look on his face. A happy look maybe, Cecil thought. A pleased look—but why would he be happy when he was so bothered by the loss of the cats?

Maybe he's happy that I'll get them back, Cecil thought. But Oscar seemed to understand that catching them again was most unlikely. Catching them the day before was tough enough.

After he had dropped off Oscar at his favorite Jasper park, where the old fellow liked to walk, Jesse helped Cecil herd cats into the net—not an easy job, herding cats—but the narrow alley between Jesse's house and the fence helped confine the cats, bunching them up so they ran from Jesse into Cecil's dip net. Within an hour, Cecil had twenty-four cats loaded among the six thirty-gallon trash cans he used for relocating cats.

"Twenty-four is close enough," Jesse declared. He had hired Cecil to catch twenty-five cats, a number he told Cecil "that is surely a quarter of the cats around the house. If we haul away more than that, the old man might notice and get after the gators again."

"Gators?" Cecil asked. "There's alligators in the neighborhood?"

"Hey, this is the Piney Woods, and we get over fifty inches of rain every year. The woods are full of swampy spots and creeks that gators love. Just down the hill on Verna there's a sorry little excuse for a creek, and plenty of alligators like it. Mostly small ones, but even those can catch a cat, and the toothy bastards do roam around. One time I saw one walking up Verna Street in the middle of the day."

Once before Jesse had hired men to haul away some cats while Oscar was away from the house. When the old man returned, Jesse told Cecil, "Oscar noticed some missing, and I covered my ass by saying the gators got them. That set the dopey old man to hunting gators."

"With a gun?" Cecil asked.

"Nah. But he hunted with evil intent and blood in his eye. Used a stick he rigged with a wire loop on the end. If he ever caught a gator with that rig, chances are he would lose a hand."

That evening Jesse invited Cecil to dinner, and he accepted, for he had traveled with Joe several times to visit Joe's uncle Jesse, so Cecil felt almost like family. At the dinner table, Oscar pushed fried chicken and potatoes around on his plate but ate nothing. "Mr. Carlson, is something wrong?" Cecil asked.

"Alligators are getting the cats again," Oscar said.

"Dang gators." Jesse seemed to be trying to hide a smile but with below par results. "Maybe in the morning, me and Cecil here can go after them along the creek. With my shotgun."

"I would prefer you not do that," Oscar said.

Oscar decided it was time to leave the dinner table. He knew Jesse was up to something with his phony offer to shoot the cat-eating gators, but what?

"Thanks for the dinner," Oscar told Jesse. "I'm too upset about the kittykens to eat much. Please excuse me." Oscar found his favorite deck chair on the screened-in porch. To his surprise, Cecil joined him, sat in the other deck chair.

"How can you tell there are cats missing?" Cecil asked.

"I know them. They are my friends."

"But you own so many cats. Can you really know who is missing? And how do you tell one cat from another?"

That, Oscar told himself, is a bad word, *own*. He sighed at the difficulty of explaining much to Cecil, who seemed good-hearted enough, but he was so young, younger than Jesse in years. But maybe a tad smarter. Maybe, Oscar thought, I can at least make him think some about the idea of one creature in this world *owning* another.

"I own no cats," he said. "They belong to themselves, same as you and me belong to ourselves and nobody owns us. I know the kittykens that choose to live here, and I can call all of them by name. A cat will answer you when you call to it. Not dogs. Talk to a dog, and it will come to you. Talk to a cat, and it will meow to you. Cats make their mewing noise only to people, did you know that? They never meow to each other or to other animals."

"Have you spoken to all your cats today?"

"I own no cats. But no. I tried, and most kittykens answered. But twenty-four of them have either wandered away from home or become meals for alligators."

Oscar watched the boy snap his head around as in disbelief at the mention of the number twenty-four, so Oscar named them. "Yes. Kittykens Thirty would not answer. Nor Kittykens Forty-Four, nor Kittykens Forty-Six." Oscar concluded with naming KittyKens Ninety-Five, and by then he had to work to stop the tears of grief and loss that stung his eyes.

"You put those in numerical order." Cecil spoke with awe in his voice. "Astounding."

"I honor them with names," Oscar said. "And they learn their names to please me and only to please me, for cats have no real need for names."

"Honor?" Cecil sounded puzzled.

Another confusing use of a word, Oscar told himself: maybe I can explain this one. But he doubted it. He decided to start with the human addiction to thought and the way thought leaped all over the place, like a monkey. "Cats," he said, "outgrow having an untamable monkey mind. As kittens, they are as bad as any human. But they mature, as we do not. Our monkey minds plague us throughout our lives, ideas of the past, of the present, of the future leaping all around in our heads, so we fail to look with diligence into the present moment. Cats could teach us about time. For all that the kittykens teach me, I honor them out of gratitude."

And I, Oscar fussed at himself, am monkey-minding myself even now into error. He clamped his eyes tight and thought of the missing cats, and he felt the tears stream down his cheeks. When he opened his eyes, he found Cecil looking at him with intensity.

"You truly love all your cats," Cecil said.

"Yes, and I can love them only because I know they are not mine."

Cecil sat back in the deck chair. "I have a confession to make, and I need to apologize."

The boy is learning, Oscar realized. But he is slow. Oscar was both pleased and troubled when Cecil told about catching the twenty-four cats and moving them to the woods beside the Angelina River. Pleased because the confession, to Oscar's thinking, showed there was some real hope the boy could learn things Jesse and most other people never managed to grasp. Pleased because the boy agreed to try to bring the cats back home.

And Oscar had to admit he was troubled because he knew Cecil could no more catch all the cats again than Oscar could catch a single alligator.

With some discomfort, Cecil eyed the woods around where he parked. Tall pines spiked the air on one side of the pickup and tangled willows grew on the other, many dipping branches into the river. "Here is where I released the cats," he said in low tones, and again he felt guilt wash over him for what his actions did to Oscar. "You know, of course, that we will catch few if any of the cats."

"I know. I'll call, and some might come."

After more than an hour of Oscar calling *kittykens, kittykens, kittykens* and Cecil managing to snare only four cats, Oscar declared it time to give up.

On the trip back to Jasper, Cecil said, "Those cats will be okay in the forest. They'll find plenty of rodents and squirrels to eat."

"Not likely," Oscar said. "Some might survive. Others, damn, there's no need for me to grieve. Others will become food for coyotes and foxes. Gators, large ones from the Angelina. Owls will get some of them. All creatures deserve to eat, however difficult I find the way some go about it."

"Jesse told me you tried to kill the alligators in your neighborhood. Vengeance for eating your cats."

"Jesse knows little of truth and even less of any value. I would never kill a gator. I hoped to snare a few and relocate them to another neighborhood, but the trick of catching them was beyond me."

"Relocating alligators," Cecil said, "could be a worse idea than moving cats."

As the pickup approached Jesse's house, Oscar said, "Rock salt."

Cecil looked at the old man. "Rock salt?"

"Jesse loads shells with rock salt for his sixteen-gauge shotgun. Sometimes he shoots at kids when they come around at night in the summer to snitch from Jesse's watermelon patch. Also in the fall when the pumpkin smashers show up around Halloween. He did hit a boy once, and the boy hollered and ran off, but nothing came of it, no angry father coming around, so I guess that rock salt didn't do any real damage to the kid. Must have stung, though."

"Thanks for the warning."

"You can stop here in the street and let out the four kittykens who chose to return with us. They'll know they're home, and you would be safer letting them go here."

Ignoring the old man's protests, Cecil drove into the driveway and stopped close to the back of the house. Oscar picked up the calico, got out of the pickup, and hurried toward the back door. Kittykens Eighteen yowled and leaped from his arms as Cecil dropped the tailgate of the pickup and set one of the trash cans on the driveway. He turned when he heard a door open, and he saw Jesse aiming a shotgun.

"No!" Oscar shouted, and Jesse fired.

For an instant the pain was so intense that Cecil expected to see his hand blown away. He lifted his arm and was surprised to see his hand intact. The back of the hand was speckled with blood, and he was relieved to see such slight wounds. After wiping his hand on his shirt in case he still had salt on his skin, he made a show of tilting the trash can so the four cats could run out.

Metallic clicking told Cecil that Jesse was reloading the shotgun. He turned to face the man.

"I told you," Jesse said. "I told you."

"I'm so sorry," Oscar said.

"Nothing here is your fault, Mr. Oscar Carlson." Cecil held up his speckled hand. "I deserve this little load of salt for taking your cats."

"I'm of half a mind to shoot you again," Jesse said.

"Do it, then." Cecil faced Jesse.

"He won't." Oscar spoke with certainty in his voice.

"He might." Cecil got into his pickup and started the engine. "Jessie is even more stupid than I used to be."

Eternal Present

When Augie Winston called to say he had the nets, the ropes, the pulleys, and the barrels, Cecil Jubak told his folks he had to go, grabbed his half-full coffee mug, and clambered into his hand-me-down Ram, eleven years old. He met Augie at the abandoned warehouse. They set to work immediately. With Augie's mechanical expertise they rigged only two pulleys and ropes for the job. The day before, they had stitched heavy casting nets together to make one giant net, which they now raised eight feet above the floor. They would return that evening at dusk, set out three dozen open cans of tuna in the middle of the massive room, and wait for cats to appear. They would stand near the pulley ropes on either side of the room, and when they judged that a majority of cats were under the net, they would yank the ropes and drop the net onto the beasts. Then, wearing heavy, elbow-length leather gloves, they would pull the cats one at a time from under the net and deliver them to one of the many barrels on the flatbed trailer Augie would bring. Where they would deliver the cats remained uncertain, but they would drive them a good twenty miles from the site.

Or at least that was the plan. But Cecil well knew that anything could go wrong, and he wondered how he had let himself be talked into yet another feral cat wrangle. But he needn't have wondered. The answer was easy. He needed the money. He'd do anything to stay away from ranch life and return to Austin. The year before, he and his best friend, Joe Jasmine, both fresh out of high school, moved there. Joe attended UT and Cecil set about starting the small subcontracting business he'd dreamed of creating. The building boom in Austin was encouraging. He had a little experience, youth, and plenty of confidence—overconfidence, as it turned out, which was soon deflated by stiff competition from far more experienced contractors with far more contacts and far more money to support their businesses.

Still, despite several offers, he stubbornly refused to take subordinate, minimum-wage jobs from his competitors and ended up slinging hash in a little diner called Lily's near campus and advertising as an expert in feral cat removal. His so-called expertise derived from an escapade of his and Joe's right before graduation from high school when they devised a way, at Joe's dad's request, to capture a couple dozen feral cats with a casting net and relocate them. Apparently, feral cats also plagued Austin, and the calls came in, sometimes for one or two cats, sometimes for as many as twenty. Then came a particularly disastrous job in Jasper that soured Cecil on the business. That old man, Oscar Carlson, was either a lunatic or a mystic, Cecil wasn't sure which. Carlson said cats have ancient souls and belong to no one. Crazy as his rants seemed, they left Cecil feeling uneasy, feeling guilty and ashamed of what he'd been doing. That's when he first seriously considered his dad's offer of working on and eventually taking over the family ranch where he'd grown up.

Cecil and Augie waited until evening to set out the tuna and post up in their appointed places. The first half hour passed with no cat sighting, but as light grew dimmer, the first cat, a lanky, scruffy tom, solid black except for one white foot, eased out from behind the corrugated metal divider, stopped, and stared at Cecil with malicious yellow eyes. Cecil's arms prickled into goose flesh. This cat could be trouble, and from the glare in those evil eyes, it could be bad trouble. Old man Carlson had spoken of cats' collective memories and their penchant for vengeance—not out of meanness, he said, but out of the natural instinct to protect their eternal present. Now cat revenge for all those relocation jobs he'd done—especially the disastrous one—stood just a few feet away, and things were likely to get ugly.

The wicked tom slunk two steps closer, ears alert, eyes fixed like lasers on Cecil's. Cecil held eye contact, hoping to stare the creature down. Another scraggly cat stepped out behind the tom, a queen, Cecil thought, and then three more from the other side of the large open doorway. One of them arched its back and hissed. Even in the warehouse heat, Cecil's goose bumps spread from his arms and stippled his chest.

The felids all stared the same wicked stare, the stare Cecil had seen so many times in this line of work. He strained to keep from blinking, and his own eyes watered from the effort, but his mind drifted elsewhere, away from the immediate fix he was in to the general fix his life was in. He desperately wanted more than eking out a rancher's living. He had spent his four years of high school plotting how to get away from Southwest Texas, away from ranch life and the ways in which it could wear a person down, embitter a person, sometimes even destroy a person physically, maybe spiritually and mentally as well. Still, it would be money in the bank, not much, but enough, and it was there waiting for him, a gift, as it were.

But he loved Austin, yearned to go back. He thought of sharing a few beers with Joe on the last evening before he headed back home. They sat in stained and tattered folding chairs salvaged from a dumpster. From the tiny patio of their second-floor apartment they looked out over the comings and goings in the parking lot. They watched a young woman with a mass of curly red hair stroll into the lot. She paused, took a quick hit off a joint, palmed it, and strolled on. God, he loved Austin. Later, three guys unloaded a keg from a shiny new F-150 and lugged it toward the building.

"Pool party," Joe said. "Want to go down?"

Cecil shook his head, raised his longneck. "This is good enough for me." They both sipped and stared out into the parking lot.

A hunter green Toyota Corolla swung into the lot. A laughing couple popped out with wet hair. They wore swim suits, hers a micro bikini. No doubt they'd been to Barton Springs.

God, he really, really loved Austin.

Cecil shook his head. He definitely needed to focus on the present, on the growing number of cats gathering in the warehouse room in which he stood. At least thirty, he estimated, and more still appearing.

They seemed in no rush to reach the tuna. They crept, they slunk, they paused to check the others' positions. The tom stayed out front and looked nowhere but at Cecil as it slowly made its way in his direction. A pair of smallish calicos—mollies, Cecil thought—stopped a step or two away from him and batted at the dangling pull-rope. He considered shooing them away but didn't want to spook the others. A glance at Augie confirmed the same dilemma. Three cats clustered near him and batted at his pull-rope.

The cat crowd had grown to fifty or more, and not one of them appeared at all interested in the open cans of tuna. The way they slunk, the way they crouched, the way they warily eyed either Cecil or Augie indicated that their interest lay in live prey, not in any processed fish mush. Bad, Cecil thought, this is really, really bad.

Again he wondered how he'd allowed himself to get involved in this mess, and again his mind wandered. Well, he remembered, he had left Austin and headed for home. As he passed through Dripping Springs, phantom pains prickled his chest and he seriously considered turning around. God, he really, really loved Austin, had since the first day they'd arrived. It felt right, felt like his future—but mostly felt like a sort of forever present. Whatever he did there, he felt fully in the moment, living the *now* without anticipating the *later*, but simultaneously feeling the future there, feeling his destiny there. He realized that his thoughts had drifted into

Oscar Carlson territory, all that yammering about the eternal present. He gritted his teeth and pressed on toward Southwest Texas.

To postpone his homecoming, he bypassed the turn-off to the family ranch and picked up Texas 131 to Tia Juanita's Restaurante y Cantina, his favorite Tex-Mex joint. Although late for the lunch crowd, he found the place packed with customers well on their way to drunk. He squeezed through to the bar. And that's where he met Augie, who had talked him into this crazy adventure. He had taken the only available bar stool.

The bartender, a good ten years older than Cecil, pushed her silky black hair off her face, and smiled. "Good to see you, Cecil."

He rose, leaned across the polished mesquite bar top, and hugged the woman's neck. He kissed her cheek. "You, too, Carmen."

She dipped her head, apparently embarrassed but pleased by the kiss. "You want a soda?"

He scowled. "Beer, Carmen, I want beer."

"I.D.?"

"You know how old I am, *mi corazón.*"

She grinned. "Only nineteen, *pequeño.*"

"*Por favor, mi amor.*" In high school, he barely got through Spanish with significant help from Joe. Just for Carmen, he committed a few of the best words to memory. He winked at her now.

She giggled. "*Sí.* Just this once." She went to fetch his beer.

"So," the man next to him said, "you're from around here."

"Used to be. I'm Cecil Jubak." He extended his hand.

"Augie Winston," the man countered and shook hands. They released their grips, but then Augie grabbed his hand again. "Wait, I know that name. You're 'The Cat Man.'"

His elbows on the bar, Cecil raised his palms and pushed his face into them. "Shit," he said. "How'd you know that?"

"Folks around here talk." Augie raised his bottle to his lips and sipped.

Carmen set a longneck in front of Cecil. "Enjoy, *chico.*"

He raised his face out of his palms. "*Gracias, señiorita bonita.*" He winked at her again. "*Was* The Cat Man," he said to Augie. "Past tense."

"I could sure use your expertise," Augie said. The construction company he worked for had bought an abandoned warehouse that would be repaired and used for equipment and materials storage. But the place was teeming with feral cats that needed to be removed first. "Nobody really knows a number," he said. "Forty, fifty, maybe a hundred."

Cecil shook his head and regretted what he was about to say. "How much?"

"Twenty per cat."

"I don't know." Cecil tapped the heel of his hand against his forehead and considered what eight hundred to two thousand dollars could mean to him. "I had this one really bad experience, you know? It really got under my skin, into my head."

"What if I get you thirty per cat?" Augie said. "And I'll help for free."

Much as he wanted to resist, Cecil couldn't pass up that money. He nodded. They tapped beer bottles as a toast to the venture. Cecil chugged his beer. He waved to Carmen down the bar and hollered, "*Señiorita bonita, dos más cervesas, por favor.*"

For the next half hour they sipped beer and discussed strategy. When Augie drained his last bottle, he set the empty on the bar, stared at the label, then said, "That one really bad experience you had, the one that got under your skin, into your head—I've got one, too. My girlfriend in Fort Worth, her name's Lily." Augie paused and scratched at his bottle's label. "She's pregnant." He stared at his bottle and shook his head. "I bolted when she told me."

"Scary stuff, huh?"

"I love her like crazy. I think about her all the time, miss her, feel guilty as hell. But, yeah, really scary stuff."

Cecil nodded but had nothing to say.

The time had come to drop the net and stop those cat bastards from doing bodily harm. Cecil signaled to Augie, who nodded stiffly.

Cecil took a slow, sliding step toward the rope and cautiously raised one hand toward it. The two calicos arched their backs and hissed, and at least twenty cats rushed in and surrounded him. The black tom crouched and looked ready to spring, and then it did spring, straight toward Cecil's chest. He stumbled backwards, tripped over the wad of cats around his feet, and went down hard. His head whacked the concrete floor. His ears rang, his vision blurred. He heard a heavy *thunk* across the room, followed by Augie's breathless voice: "Shit!"

And then the net came down. Still dazed, Cecil didn't immediately register what had happened, but slowly he recognized the feel of heavy mesh across his face. He attempted to rise, but his muscles felt atrophied, weighted down. Cats, all outside the net, lay on his legs, their claws clutching his jeans, some of them pressing hard against his flesh. They sat or lay across his arms and stomach. As his eyes began to focus, he looked directly into the wicked yellow eyes of the tom. It sat on his chest, its chin directly over his, and stared down into his eyes. He felt helpless to do anything but stare back.

He would have sworn at that moment that the cat spoke to him. Not out loud, but through its eyes somehow, through some sort of telepathic transference into his eyes and down into his brain receptors. "Leave us," it said. "We do not belong to you." Cecil knew he was hallucinating, but that's what old man Carlson had said: cats belong to no one. That crack on the head had addled him. "Leave us," he felt the tom say. "Go and follow your bliss."

Follow your bliss? What kind of crazy, New Agey bullshit was that for a cat to say?

"Go to your eternal present. Leave us."

He badly needed help, Cecil knew. That head whack had done serious damage. Still, he also remembered driving away from Austin and thinking that it felt like his present and his future simultaneously. He closed his eyes to block out the cat's words.

He awoke sometime later, maybe a minute, maybe ten. The cats were gone. He heard Augie thrashing and cursing furiously. Rather than following suit, he pushed himself up far enough to lean on his right forearm, clutched the net with his left hand, and began scooching toward the edge and pulling the net at the same time. Out from under it, he eased to a sitting position and checked Augie's progress: still thrashing and cursing, he had almost reached the net's edge. Cecil pushed up onto his feet and wobbled on rubbery legs. He shuffled to the corrugated wall and leaned against it. Night had settled in completely, and the room was pitch black. With the wall for support, he inched slowly toward the warehouse door.

Outside, he clutched the door frame and waited for Augie.

When Augie joined him, they linked arms for support and hobbled toward Augie's truck, where they plopped onto the edge of the flatbed. Cecil felt cat hair on his tongue. He leaned over and spat.

Augie did the same. They remained silent for some time, and then Augie said, "Holy shit!"

Cecil nodded. "Yeah?"

Augie sucked in a deep breath, exhaled it audibly. "I'm going home. Back to Fort Worth." He paused, chuckled, then added, "To my beautiful Lily and my beautiful unborn baby."

"Sounds good."

"It's where I belong, Cecil. It's my eternal present."

Cecil's head snapped up and he peered at Augie. "Wait. Why'd you use that expression, *eternal present*?"

Augie started to speak, then shrugged and stared at the ground for several seconds. He shook his head. "I don't know. Forget it. I'm going home, that's all. What about you?"

Cecil knew the answer. First, he would get to a clinic to get his head checked, and then he would head back to Austin. He would take one of those minimum-wage jobs with a contractor, learn the business inside and out, and eventually break away and start his own subcontracting business.

"Me," he said, "I'm going home, too. Back to Austin. Back to *my* eternal present."

Augie stared at him and frowned, but then tilted his head back and laughed. Cecil laughed, too, and they high-fived.

Things Roman

As he walked down to the river, Cecil Jubak couldn't help a rueful smile at the irony of it all. He guessed it was tough for most parents-to-be to decide whether they'd rather have a baby girl or a baby boy. But for Cecil—who luck, or God, or the merciless math of the gene pool had thrust into the role of grandparent-to-be this time around—the answer had always been clear: have boys, not girls.

Have boys, not girls was not a matter of favoritism for Cecil. He had nothing at all against other men's daughters, and he certainly wasn't one to hold a grudge against his own. It was just that boys were so much easier to raise. Boys were less emotional, they required less money in their free time, and they were less whiney. And when it came to the worry factor surrounding the three-letter word that had come to occupy more and more of Cecil's waking hours since his own daughters had reached dating age, there was no comparison—boys scoring about a one on his ten-point worry scale and girls at least a thirty-seven.

Have boys, not girls was not a matter of blind prejudice. Cecil could see that he was unfair. But as the births of Venus, Minerva, and Diana had reminded him in turn, life was unfair. He sat down in his green plastic thinking chair and watched the river flow past the weather-beaten wood of his boat dock, feeling again the sad desperation that had grown to fill his heart as hope for a son had faded. This time it was a grandson his heart yearned to see delivered, but that didn't make his desire for a blue-swaddled bundle any less poignant. A male offspring had become for him like a desert mirage for a cowboy dying of thirst. And having grown up working on his father's cattle ranch outside Jordan, Texas, Cecil knew what a desert mirage looked like. In his imagination he gazed wistfully upon a strapping young man with whom he could share the wealth of arcane knowledge he'd gleaned since leaving the cactus-cursed desert plains for the river-blessed Hill Country: the tail-slap of a gar off the bow of the canoe, the croaking cough of a great blue heron startled off the nest, the sweet swish of a perfect swing chasing the ball as it arced off the tee.

Cecil's wife Juno said it was all a matter of luck. *Fortuna Brevis* was the term she used—a Latin phrase she said meant "fickle fortune" and referred to one aspect of the Roman goddess Fortuna, to whom the women of ancient Rome had prayed during childbirth and for whom Juno had wanted to name their third baby girl. But when Cecil found out that Fortuna was later connected with women of ill fame, he'd asked for a

85

goddess of higher moral character and preferably some association with the great outdoors. Juno obliged by naming the child after the goddess Diana, who she said was also connected with childbirth, as well as with chastity—an irony that Juno would point out to Cecil more than once over the course of Diana's junior year in high school, and that he would come to appreciate in the fullness of time. Juno Jubak was as lovely and well-educated a lady as any who ever lived, and Cecil wouldn't trade her for a houseful of strapping sons. But like her mother, her grandmother, and the rest of her female-centric family, Juno had a strange fascination with all things Roman and a wildly emotional reaction to childbirth.

Indeed, it was this hysterical quality that was the first and most important reason Cecil was convinced it was better to have boys than girls. Boys were naturally less emotional about the problems that came their way, and this was strengthened as they grew by a society that viewed emotion as a mostly female trait. Anyway, it seemed that way to Cecil. For example, if a boy had a derogatory comment made about him at school—like he was pregnant, for instance; well, no ... like maybe he had no balls—he would simply get into a fight with the offender. After a few punches, the problem would be solved. Girls, on the other hand, required much more emotional attention, as their natural reaction to the same situation would be to cry and then gossip. This would escalate into a huge problem between the girls involved, which would eventually result in more crying, which would occur at home where it would be the parents' job to deal with it. At San Saba High School, for instance, where all three of Cecil's lovely daughters had been on the Armadillos cheerleading squad—Venus and Minerva having since moved on to the university and become Longhorns, Tri-Delts, and Classics majors like their mother before them—a vicious rumor had gone around that the weight Diana, who was now nearing the end of her junior year, started putting on back during football season was due to pregnancy. The cheerleading uniforms were white, which of course emphasized the weight gain, with purple-and-gold pompoms that did not serve well to soak up tears during crying jags. Cecil's entire month of November had been spent trying to calm Diana's alternating fits of despair and bouts of rage—during which tear-soaked purple-and-gold pompoms were hurled across the living room with great frequency but little practical effect—while Diana alternately sobbed and snarled, "I swear to God it's just a rumor," into her cell phone, and Juno talked wistfully about irony and how quickly *Fortuna Brevis* could regress into *Fortuna Mala*.

Cecil shifted a little in his thinking chair and glanced up at the house, rebuilt out of native limestone in an imposing style that Juno had identified as Romanesque, after the last house—built in equally imposing Romanesque style out of wood, and the birthplace of Juno's grandmother and great-grandmother—had been destroyed in the great flood of 1938. It was not Cecil's home. Not really. He had married into it, and into the vast tract of acreage on the Colorado River that went with the Romanesque limestone manor. So he'd not been offended earlier that afternoon when his mother-in-law, Vesta, shooed him out the door and across the porch—Juno and Vesta called it a *portico*—with childbirth-hysterics already creeping into her voice. This was something Cecil was used to, Juno having insisted on giving birth to all three of their children in her own home, as her mother had done before her. And now, despite all her cell-phone-snarled protestations to the contrary, it was Diana's turn.

No, it was better to leave the house to the women—Vesta, Juno, Diana, the midwife—and retreat instead to the river out back, the one place on earth where Cecil truly felt at home. He had already gutted out three rollercoaster rides of boy-hope and girl-dread right here on this boat dock, in this same chair, watching the river roll by and hoping that instead of a pink swaddling blanket emerging from the back door, he would see a blanket of blue. His canoe lay upside-down on the carpet grass sward above him. A bucket of golf balls and his bag of clubs sat at his feet. These were the same companions he'd had for each of his previous experiences with labor. And even though this time it was his daughter, rather than his wife, who was having the baby, Cecil was far from panicked. He had the means to keep himself entertained.

Indeed, this was the second reason that Cecil was convinced it was better to have boys than girls. Boys did not require money to entertain themselves throughout their childhood, adolescence, and even adulthood. They could amuse themselves in clever and creative ways with almost anything. They could whittle sticks into baseball bats; make mud into paste, pies, or projectiles; and fashion countless other common materials into virtually anything. When boys reached high school age, all they needed was a rusted-out old truck and a job that would provide money to fix up said truck. Despite the myriad chores that came along with growing up on a cattle ranch, as a teenager Cecil managed to hustle and scrape together enough odd jobs to turn his pop's beat-up old castoff ranch truck into a red rocket that struck fear into the hearts of the street-racing crowd at Jordan High—and not a penny of that hard-earned cash had come out of his father's pocket. Girls, on the other hand, had to have money or toys that cost money. They required dolls and doll houses when they were young, and money to go to the mall when they were a little older. And then there were the cell phones. Cecil shuddered, remembering the cell phone bills Diana had racked up as "I swear to God it's just a rumor" regressed into "I'm going to raise the baby myself." More than $2000 in three months. What boy, Cecil asked himself, would ring up a bill like that?

He would never forget the day Diana introduced them to the father of her coming child—Cecil had heard Diana call him her "baby daddy" on her cell phone—a long, lanky Longhorn freshman named Frankie who she met while visiting her sisters in Austin and who Cecil had come to think of as Frankie the Snake. Cecil interrupted a rambling explanation of their future plans—or rather, the lack thereof—that he chiefly remembered for the repeated phrases "not in a relationship" and "no plans to marry" with the question: "Do you have a cell phone, Frankie?"

"Can't afford one," Frankie said. "I'm paying my own way through college on a baseball scholarship. Diana always calls me on my dorm phone. Why?"

Cecil levered himself up out of his green plastic thinking chair and whispered a fervent prayer to the Goddess Fortuna—although he was neither a Roman nor a woman—that this time the childbirth he awaited would result in a boy, not a girl. Juno had told him on more than one occasion that the sign of Fortuna's favor was a cornucopia. Cecil didn't have a cornucopia, but he did have a bucket of balls and a golf bag full of clubs which, it seemed to him, strongly resembled a cornucopia. And it came to him almost like a vision that a hole-in-one would be a sign from the goddess that the birth of a male offspring was finally at hand.

He picked up his golf bag and his bucket of balls and stepped up onto the carpet grass. He looked out across the river, trying to gauge the width of the stream. It looked like the water was down about a foot from the level it had hit after the last rains, but was still flowing muddy and wide—about thirty yards, he guessed. He pulled the sand wedge from his bag, dropped three balls onto the fairway-high grass, lined up the shot, and swung through the first ball.

He could feel that the shot was short even before he saw it arc shallowly up over the river and splash into the muddy water about five yards shy of the opposite bank. He shook his head, replaced the sand wedge, pulled out the pitching wedge. Then he lined up the shot and swung through the second ball, watching the arc of its trajectory carry across the river to plop into the mud on the far side.

Short again. He shook his head, replaced the pitching wedge, and pulled out the nine iron. Then he lined up the shot and swung through the third ball, watching the arc of its trajectory carry across the river to bounce up off the back of the close-clipped carpet grass green on the far side and disappear into the pecan trees behind it.

Long. He dumped the bucket, whispered another fervent prayer, and took his time sending each ball in turn arcing across the river. Some of them bounced up off the back of the green and into the pecan trees. Others bit on the back of the green. But not a single shot came within easy putting distance of the pin—much less dropping in for a hole-in-one. When he finished the bucket, he picked up his golf bag and threw it into the river. Then he sat down in his thinking chair and tried to gauge the strength of the current while he contemplated women, luck, golf, rivers, and God.

Rivers had been lucky for Cecil, mostly. They had introduced him to women, improved his golf game, and brought him closer if not to God then to Creation at least. The day after he graduated high school, Cecil fled his father's brushcountry cattle ranch for the city of Austin to work construction during the boom. He arrived tanned and fit and wise enough in the ways of women to keep his mouth shut and listen while Juno talked about ancient Rome. He'd met her on the Colorado River during her time as a Longhorn, a Tri-Delt, and a Classics major—literally ramming his boat into the one she was riding in so he could get the chance to make it up to her by buying her dinner—and courted her on riverside picnics at Auditorium Shores. Marrying Juno gave him the farm in San Saba County that she'd grown up on and that they made thrive together, a collaboration in the truest and best sense: tireless physical labor on his part, unshakably patient guidance on hers, and lifegiving water from the river that made their peanuts and pecans flourish. When Cecil had time and the water was high enough, he packed his canoe with camping gear and ran the fifty-three miles of Colorado that lay between his boat dock and the free LCRA boat ramp at Cedar Point on Lake Buchanan. He'd grown to know every bend and trouble-spot, every sand spit and fishing hole. He'd grown to know the peace that came from paddling beneath towering limestone cliffs and circling bald eagles. But even so, the Colorado sometimes managed to surprise him. Like women and luck, the river was always changing.

Diana was the only one of his daughters Cecil ever managed to talk into running the river with him. She was thirteen years old at the time, still a little gangly but beginning to blossom into the graceful beauty that she would later come to inhabit with her mother and sisters. As they paddled away from the boat dock—Cecil in the aft seat with the ice chest and water container, and Diana in the bow with her cell phone—Cecil felt sure he was finally on the verge of sharing the precious peace of the wild river with someone he loved. His hopes were dashed, though, by the lack of cell towers. In order to convince Diana to undertake the trip, he had to promise her cell service on every gravel bar and sand spit between their boat dock and the LCRA boat ramp. But he could only deliver on this promise at Flat Rock in Bend, hardly a day into their three-day trip—and even then, she could hardly hear. So his heavenly vision of shared peace on the river deteriorated into a hell of constant complaining that could best be described as a perpetual whine.

Indeed, this very whininess was the third reason that Cecil was convinced it was better to have boys than girls. Whining was bad enough when girls were very young; but once adolescence had been reached, the problem quickly escalated out of control. Adolescent girls would whine at the drop of a pin and would complain to anyone or anything that crossed their paths. Sadly, the problem persisted throughout most of adulthood as well, although it was greatly diminished—except during pregnancy. Boys, on the other hand, were much less inclined to whine and were easily made to stop their bellyaching if and when the occasional fit did occur. They were generally easygoing and carefree, no matter what came their way. A lack of cell towers would never cause a boy to whine on the river. Come to think of it, Cecil realized, no self-respecting boy would even bring a cell phone into a canoe.

At the thought of the canoe, Cecil sat bolt upright in his chair. He had suddenly remembered Juno telling him that, in addition to a cornucopia, the favor of Fortuna—who was sometimes represented with a boat rudder—could also be shown by the lucky guiding of a ship. Cecil had thrown his golf-bag cornucopia into the river in frustration at the lack of a sign that his earlier prayer might be answered. Maybe if he could guide his boat to the spot where the golf bag rested, and rescue the bag from the river bottom, it would be a sign that his heartfelt plea for a boy might be answered after all.

In a flash, Cecil fetched a paddle and a boathook, and lowered his bright green canoe into the water. "Oh, Goddess Fortuna," he prayed as he paddled, "send me a grandson. End my years of boy-despair." He paddled and prayed, prayed and paddled, until he was directly upstream from the spot where he figured the golf bag had struck the water. Then he switched the paddle for the boathook, which he lowered and used to dredge the river bottom as the canoe was carried downstream.

He came up with nothing but mud and weeds. But he kept paddling and praying, praying and paddling, fighting the current to get above the spot where his best judgment said the golf bag would've drifted to the bottom, then lowering the boathook and dredging for a golf-bag-sized snag.

Nothing again. And again. And yet again.

Until finally, so exhausted from paddling and dredging that he could hardly make his way back to the boat dock, Cecil was forced to admit defeat. He rolled the canoe as he climbed out of it, feeling so fatigued as he dragged himself out of the water that all he could do was watch his beloved ship sink to the bottom in the shallows just offshore—where it lay barely visible in the murk like the shadowy face of a hostile god.

Cecil lay on the weather-beaten wood of the boat dock, soaked and breathing heavy, and feeling completely betrayed by women, luck, golf, rivers, and God. The only thing that hadn't let him down was his faithful chair. But in a fit of rage born out of a mix of girl-frustration and boy-despair, he lurched to his feet and lobbed the green plastic chair as far as he could into the muddy water.

Then he turned his back on river, golf bag, canoe, and chair—in short, on all he had come to think of as his—and faced the back side of the Romanesque limestone mansion he'd married into. As he sat there dripping, empty, at the end of himself, Cecil saw Juno emerge from the back door with a blue-swaddled bundle.

He hardly had the strength to sob for joy.

Mexico

The rising sun smeared the sky blood-red, stained the coming thunderheads into mounds of raw meat roiling up off the Gulf. The south wind whooshed through the catclaw and mesquite thicket Beau Mulebach was making slow progress through, the horse limping along behind him as the first heavy drops of rain started to fall.

"Easy there, old man," Beau said as the horse spooked, jerking back against the reins in his hand. "It's just a hurricane is all." He turned, stroked Mexico's neck, rubbed the bony outcrop of withers beneath the saddle horn.

The horse nudged Beau, pressing him back toward the left stirrup, and he couldn't help but smile despite the nature of their errand and the big weather coming on. Pushing thirty years old now, snaggle-toothed and arthritis-bent, Mexico was once as game a brush-popper as there'd ever been and the best roping horse in Southwest Texas—as devil-may-care as the man who'd spent his life in the saddle Beau strapped on before daybreak: Rooster Stiles, for Beau's money the greatest all-around cowboy who ever lived.

"One last ride?" He scratched the base of the bay's mane. "I don't know about that." In the bloody half-light he took in Mexico's swollen knees, his legs gnarled like the storm-bent mesquites the two of them stood among, his wasted muscles. Beau had led the horse all the way from the old Jubak stables—Mulebach stables now, although that was still hard to wrap his head around—to the thicket they stood in now, a distance of almost a mile. Saddled and bridled, yes. But only as a gesture of respect on this final trip into the brush. "We'd best walk this last bit."

He felt Mexico nudge him again, urging him to mount. As if the horse knew about the pistol in the saddlebag, knew the reason the two of them were here. And against his better judgment, Beau snugged his hat down tight and swung up into Rooster Stiles's saddle, feeling Mexico stagger forward, the branches crackling and popping as thorns snagged Beau's shirt and jeans and the wind snatched at his hat. He'd dreamed of sitting in this saddle since he was eight years old, watching Rooster beat Rex Marshall in the thousand-dollar roping match that had cost Rex a finger and become a legend in Southwest Texas. But this wasn't the way Beau had envisioned his first time on the hurricane deck of Rooster's big bay stallion—a stumbling, one-way ride to a mercy killing.

The rain was coming down harder now, stinging his face like the catclaw branches. But it was welcome. A drought-breaking rain, despite the flooding and tornadoes that were predicted to come with it, a rain to refill empty lakes and get the Frio River—that had run completely dry—flowing again. The best the old horse could manage was a lopsided half-lope that joggled Beau in the saddle as they burst out of the thicket into a patch of fire-blackened prickly pear grazed almost to the ground by his hungry cattle. He'd seared the spines off the nopales with a pear-burner the week before because the grass was gone, the brindle crossbred cows that usually ran at the sight of a man afoot following close behind him through the August heat, descending on the cactus leaves the minute the flames scorched them bare of thorns. He knew that the rain would send green shoots of native grama and bluestem grass sprouting again, provide planting moisture for pastures of coastal Bermuda, make possible a new start for this brush-country land that was newly his. And in the spring he'd buy the beginnings of a herd of registered Black Angus that would vault this nineteenth-century holdover of a cattle ranch into the modern era.

But first, he told himself, he had to make an ending.

It had been coming for six months now, that ending, since the day he and Cecil Jubak sat down with the banker and signed the papers to make the old Jubak ranch Beau's. To celebrate, he'd walked out of the Jordan State Bank and paid May Belle Stiles a thousand dollars—that should've been spent on fixing fences and building pens, clearing brush and seeding pastures—for Rooster's horse and saddle. As he worked to modernize the Jubak place he'd bought when Cecil's father died, and integrate it with the Mulebach ranch he'd inherited when his own father passed, Beau watched the equine arthritis worsen despite the pampering he gave the horse: Mexico's stride shortening more every day, his back hollowing, his knees twisting so bad he could barely bend them. The last thing Beau had wanted to do at five o'clock this morning was crawl out of his and Wanda's bed in the old Jubak house that they were still settling into and lead Mexico into the brush to put a bullet in his brain. But Beau couldn't bear to see the horse suffer even one more day, and cleaning up after the hurricane that was blowing in would have to occupy his full attention—or the future he was birthing for the ranch and for his family would die stillborn.

It was as if the horse had known all along where they were headed. Mexico staggered through a thicket of huisache and guajillo into the once-grassy, now barren, vega where Beau had spent the last three mornings digging a grave broad enough to hold a horse and deep enough so the starving coyotes couldn't dig up the body. It was in this very spot that Rooster Stiles had died of a heart attack almost twenty years ago, in the saddle Beau sat in now, riding after outlaw cattle at the Jubaks' fall round-up. He brought the horse up next to the mound of dirt he'd left at the edge of the pit and dismounted, draping the saddlebag over his shoulder as he led Mexico down the gentle slope to join Rooster at that big rodeo in the sky.

"Well done, old man," Beau said, stroking the horse's neck that felt warm after their ride despite the rain that was slashing sideways in sheets now and the wind that was howling. "I should've known all along you had it in you."

He opened the saddlebag and pulled out the cow horn necklace that Rooster had given him at his first roundup, and that Rooster's mentor, Old Man Merriweather, had given Rooster at his. The horn was black, about the length of a grown man's fingers, with a silver cap at the base and a wicked point at the business end. Old Man Merriweather had sawed it off the outlaw cow that gutted his horse in an epic brush-battle that had become as much the stuff of legend as Rooster's thousand-dollar roping match. The horsehair braid that served as a chain had been cut from the dead horse's tail after the mercy killing. It had once been blonde, almost white; but Beau had taken black hair from Mexico's mane and extended the length of the braid so it would stretch around the horse's neck. And he put it there now, reaching up and tying it carefully. Beau had worn that good luck charm to every roping match and rodeo, every roundup and cattle-working he'd been a part of since the day he'd gotten it from Rooster, and he was loathe to let it go. But the time had come to return it.

"Before I do this," Beau said, looking deep into the horse's soft brown eyes, "I need you to know why. It's better for a greatheart like you to go out clean than to waste away so stove up he can't even move. I couldn't let May Belle send you off to the kill auction in Stephenville, then on that awful trailer ride to the Beltex slaughterhouses in Juarez. Don't get me wrong. It ain't May Belle's fault that she had to part ways with you. She couldn't keep you up anymore. I thought I might be able to pamper you, make you game as a green-broke colt for a little while. But turning back time is beyond my power. This thing I'm about to do, it's the right thing to do."

He reached into the saddlebag, and grasping the pistol, leaned his face against the horse's face, breathing into Mexico's nose with his nose and scratching the horse's whiskery chin. As he felt Mexico relax, Beau stroked the horse's broad forehead, counting the distance of four fingers down the midline. Then he eased the pistol up out of the saddlebag and into the kill spot, closed his eyes, and squeezed the trigger.

The explosion left Beau deaf and smelling burnt gunpowder, and when he opened his eyes after the longest moment of his life, the ringing in his ears was still so fierce he could hardly hear the storm. The horse lay peaceful and still as though he were sleeping. The cow horn necklace rested against his chest, the silver shining back the red half-light, and all of a sudden Beau found himself remembering Rooster's funeral. He saw again the sea of hatband-creased foreheads bowed in prayer and Rooster lying there in that casket looking so small, the same way Mexico looked lying here in a homemade grave slowly filling with rain.

And it seemed to Beau, as he put the pistol back into the saddlebag and picked up the shovel, that instead of up off the Gulf, the hurricane had come howling straight out of the Book of Revelation. He felt the wind take his hat as he started shoveling, not knowing whether the wetness on his face was tears or blood, or whether he was making an ending or a beginning.

III. Dead Dogs and Redemption

Dead Dogs

One month after I turned twelve and got my chocolate lab Bo, old man Needham shot that puppy dead. We lived on the ranch immediately neighboring Needham's place. I took Bo out for a romp on our place, and after about half an hour, a big jackrabbit spooked a few feet from us. Bo tore after it, me running behind yelling until I was hoarse for Bo to stop. He paid no mind, and when that jack zipped under the fence bordering Needham's place, Bo scrambled under right behind him. By the time I got to the fence, they were out of sight in cedar and mesquite. I tried climbing over, snagged my pants on the barbed wire, and finally figured out I could make it easier by following the example of the jack and Bo. I hit the ground and rolled under, then popped upright and kept running, hollering after Bo the whole time, him barking like mad somewhere ahead of me.

Then I heard the pop of a small-caliber rifle and Bo went silent. I screamed his name and fought my way through a tangle of cedar and mesquite, until I hit a clearing. Maybe seventy yards ahead, Bo lay on the ground and old man Needham stood over him, a twenty-two rifle in his hands. When I got close, I skidded to Bo's side, scuffing the Justin boots I'd also gotten for my birthday. Blood oozed from a small hole just behind his front left shoulder, and his eyes had already begun to glaze.

I looked up at the old man. "Why'd you shoot him?" I screamed.

He glared. "Can't have no sheep-killing dog running free, boy."

"He's not a sheep-killer, you bastard. You son-of-a-bitching bastard!" I was crying by then. I lay my head against Bo's shoulder and slid my hands underneath to cradle him.

Needham grinned, not happy, just mean, and spat a stream of snuff juice right in front of my knee, and it splashed onto my jeans. "You got spunk, boy. And you better use it now." He spat again, the stream that time hitting me square on one knee. "You want that sheep-killer's dead body, you better grab it fast." He rotated his head to look back at his truck, maybe fifteen or twenty steps away. "I'm going back to that truck to exchange this twenty-two for a high-powered pellet gun. If you're still in range, you're going to get a pellet or two in your ass." He grinned again and turned to stride toward the truck.

I couldn't lift Bo from my kneeling position. I staggered to my feet, then bent and scooped him up with some effort. The old man had already reached his truck and opened the driver's side door. I turned and ran, the weight of Bo slowing me down significantly. I yelped when I felt the sting in my left butt cheek, and I yelped again when the right cheek got the same treatment, but I kept running. Just before I hit the cover of cedars and mesquites, I yelped once more when the right cheek got another dose. Then I was clear of that bastard with the pellet gun.

And from that moment forward, I wanted revenge.

Back home, I discovered that the first shot had torn through my jeans, and the pellet had lodged in my flesh. My mom pulled it out with tweezers, daubed the spot with iodine, and taped a square of gauze over it. The second shot, when I was farther away, had penetrated my jeans but not my skin, on which it left an angry red spot sure to bruise. The third had done little damage, even to my jeans.

While Mom doctored me, I sobbed, not because of pain but because of Bo. My dad listened to the story, his teeth clenched, his hands squeezing into fists, releasing, then squeezing again.

"I'll be back in a bit," he said flatly.

Mom looked up at him from where she worked on my wounds. Her brows furrowed. "It's Wacy Needham, Robert. You're dancing on barbed wire." What she meant was that Needham was a known asshole who wouldn't take kindly to complaints. He'd never apologize or make amends. More likely, he'd pull a gun or take a swing at Dad. "Just call the sheriff," Mom said.

Dad shook his head. "Bo was on his property. All Needham would have to do is say the dog was chasing his sheep or a calf. Nobody, not even the sheriff, would blame him for the shooting." His jaw muscles bulged when he gritted his teeth. He turned and strode out of the room.

An hour or so later when he returned, I lay on my stomach dozing on the couch. He looked pale, and when he laid his hand on my shoulder, I felt it shaking. "Can you get up?"

"Did you talk to him?"

"Yes."

"And?"

"Just let it go."

"I won't," I said.

"Can you get up?"

"Yes, sir."

"All right. Come on."

I hobbled behind him to the tool shed, which he kept organized better than most hardware stores. He handed me a shovel and picked Bo up from where we had left him near the shed. Bo looked stiff in his arms.

I fought back tears. Under the blinding July sun, Dad walked to a far corner of what passed for our back yard, enclosed by a short picket fence. He laid Bo down gently, took the shovel from me, and began to dig. Lack of rain had hardened the dirt, but he grunted and dug until the hole was maybe four feet deep. He eased Bo in and handed me the shovel. Once I had managed three or four scoops, he finished the burial. The armpits of his shirt had dark circles, and he dragged the sleeve of his right arm across his sweating forehead.

"That's it," he said. He stared down at the fresh mound of dirt.

I was crying. "You should have shot that old man," I said. "Bastard. He's a son-of-a-bitching bastard!"

He clenched his jaw, and I could see hurt in his eyes, too, but all he said was, "Watch your mouth, son." And then he ambled back toward the house.

"Bastard!" I screamed toward him, the back of his shirt damp like the armpits.

I spent the next week moping around the house, pretending my butt hurt worse than it did, and avoiding eye contact or conversation with my dad, whom I felt pretty sure I hated for not taking a stronger stand. And I obsessed about how to get revenge on old man Needham. I had to plan carefully because he was a tough old bastard infamous throughout the county for his meanness and recalcitrance.

Needham was fourth-generation owner of about fifteen-hundred acres with cattle, a few sheep, and three pump jacks. He also leased part of the place to hunters in the fall. He'd beaten the ever-loving hell out of three hunters who didn't see any bucks on a weekend hunt and demanded their money back. They pressed charges, but their contract clearly stated that payment was not dependent on a successful hunt, and Needham claimed they threatened him and he beat them in self-defense. He was, to say the least, anti-social, and he had lived alone on his place for the past twelve years. He'd been married four times. One wife left him within a year of discovering what ranch life was like. One he apparently beat occasionally, and she divorced him after they had two boys. She took the boys with her, and none of them ever contacted him again. Another lasted about eight years and then ran off with some man he'd hired to haul cattle to auction. After three years, the last one shot him in his left shoulder, supposedly aiming for his heart, and reportedly sat in prison somewhere with no regrets. Worst of all, as far as I was concerned, he had killed my dog Bo.

Old man Needham deserved to die, and I thought really hard about doing the honors.

But how not to get caught was the question. I needed help, so I told my mom I felt better and wondered if my friend Cody could come over. His mom brought him the next morning, and my mom invited her in for coffee and gossip. I said we were going fishing. The tank was the lowest it had ever been and probably lousy for fishing, but Mom didn't seem to think of that. She just nodded vaguely that it was okay with her.

Outside, Cody said, "I get the blue rod," and trotted ahead of me toward the tool shed, where Dad kept all the fishing equipment. He had already flung open the door and stepped inside by the time I got there.

I passed the door. "Come on," I said.

He ducked his head out the door. "What about the rods?"

"Come on."

He shut the door and followed me to the back of the shed. I plopped down and leaned against the wall. It was shady there and the little breeze relieved the heat of midmorning. We couldn't see the house, which meant our moms couldn't see us either, and better yet it was out of their earshot even if they happened to step outside. We could, however, see the freshly turned dirt where Bo was buried. I looked away, down between my scuffed boots.

Cody sat in the dirt beside me and shoved my shoulder. "Marcus, what's up?"

"I need help."

"With what?"

"Revenge. On old man Needham."

"You gonna kill him?"

I dug one boot heel into the dirt while I thought about that. "Nah, I guess not."

"What then?"

"Something," I said. "A taste of his own medicine." I picked up a stone and threw it at an oak trunk fifteen yards away. I missed. I shifted my weight and winced. The spot where that one pellet had penetrated my flesh still hurt some. "Hey," I said, "you know anyone with a pellet gun?"

He shook his head, but then his face brightened. "Wait. Gordon Mims has one."

"Gordon hates me."

"Gordon hates everybody. But I'll bet you money if we told him what it was for and let him come along, he'd let us use the gun."

I considered that but finally shook my head. "Nobody else can know. Too risky."

He shrugged. We sat for a while silently thinking. He chunked a couple of rocks at the tree and hit it both times. Eventually, he tilted his chin toward that fresh-turned dirt. "Is that Bo?" I nodded but didn't look. "Man," he said, "I'm really sorry."

We sat again in silence until he suddenly slapped my shoulder. "We're so stupid, Marcus."

"What?"

"Old man Needham's dog. You know, that border collie with one white eye and one brown."

I frowned. "What about him?"

He punched my shoulder. "A taste of his own medicine. How do you think the old man would feel if his dog got shot?"

It took me only a few seconds to process his point. "Cody, you're a genius!"

He gave me a well-that's-obvious look. "Well, yeah."

I remembered hearing the pop of old man Needham's twenty-two and running straight to where he was, Bo bleeding on the ground in front of him. "I don't know," I said. "Maybe too risky. Guns make noise and attract attention. And anyway, he'd know who did it."

"Jeez!" Cody said and slapped his forehead. "You want revenge but you don't want to kill the old man and you don't want to borrow Gordon's pellet gun and you don't want to shoot that dog." He shook his head. "I'm done. No more ideas."

"Rats!" I said.

"Yeah," he said. "Damn!"

I clutched his upper arm. "No, rats. Real rats."

He scrunched up his face. "What about them?"

"We get them sometimes. In the shed, in the wood pile, even in the attic."

"So?"

"So Dad keeps a bunch of poison for when it happens."

His eyes brightened. He held up his hand for a high-five. "Now who's the genius?" We slapped hands.

Like most folks who lived on ranches around there, we kept the pantry and freezer stocked so we didn't have to make too many forty-mile round trips into Brownwood for shopping. Cody and I decided hamburger would be best for mixing poison in. That determined, I spent two weeks spying on old man Needham's house, recording his comings and goings. Cody joined me on days his mom agreed to bring him out. The old man kept a pretty regular schedule of feeding livestock, checking fence lines, and whatever other ranch business he tended to. He always took his border collie along. It rode in the front seat, its left shoulder pressed against his right. As tight as they were, I figured that dog had to be as mean as the old man, and I knew killing it would be the perfect revenge.

But what really got our attention was that two Saturdays in a row he left the house about ten in the morning without the dog, and he didn't return by the time we grew tired of watching, usually about two. We agreed that the following Saturday was our target date.

On Thursday, I snuck a pound of hamburger out of the freezer and four boxes of poison pellets out of the shed. I hid both in my bedroom closet, behind some sweaters I wouldn't be wearing for months to come. Later, when the burger was thawed, I crushed the pellets as best I could and kneaded then into the meat. I stuffed the mixture into a sandwich bag, sealed it, and dropped it back behind the sweaters.

Friday afternoon, I realized my mistake. The burger had already begun to spoil, and despite the sealed sandwich bag the smell seeped into my room. I copped a plastic container from the kitchen, closed the bag into it, sprayed the room with some of Mom's air freshener, and prayed neither of my folks came to my room.

Saturday morning, Cody's mom got him there a little after ten. We kicked around the house casually for half an hour before saying we were going to the tank to fish. I fetched the container of burger and stuffed it under my shirt.

Cody and I hiked the fence line to just about the same spot where the jack rabbit, Bo, and I had scrambled under, and then we plodded a half-mile or so to Needham's house. We approached from the back, hoping like hell that the old man had maintained the pattern we had observed the previous two Saturdays. The yard was fenced with chain link. Just outside the fence grew a tangle of prickly pear and scrub mesquite. We picked our way through it and reached the fence about midway between each corner. We didn't see the dog but speculated that either old man Needham had taken him along or he was just hanging out in the front yard waiting for his master's return. I slipped the container out from my shirt.

"Wait," Cody said. "We should drop it in a corner."

He was right. It wouldn't be as noticeable to Needham in case the dog hadn't eaten it before he returned. Once the dog ate it, there would be no evidence at all. We squeezed between the fence and the mesquite and cactus until we reached the corner. I opened the box and almost gagged at the smell of the rotting meat. But I held my breath, pulled the meat out of the bag, formed it into a fat ball, and dropped it over the fence. Then we squeezed our way back toward the middle where we knew we could get through the prickly mess of cactus and mesquite. Just before we reached our spot, the dog started barking from somewhere in front of the house.

"Shit," Cody said. "Go, go!" He lunged into the mass of growth.

Clutching the chain link for stability, I inched along toward the same spot. When that dog rounded the house corner, he skidded to a stop and quit barking. He eyed us briefly and then sprinted toward the fence barking.

"Come on," Cody shouted back. "Move, move!"

But I couldn't. Terrified, I watched that dog close in, convinced that it was as vicious as Needham. I imagined it jumping over the fence, or even breaking through it, and snacking on pieces of our legs it bit off as we tried to run. But my fear froze me in place. I couldn't even unclench my fingers from the chain link. When he reached me, he reared up on hind legs and pressed his forepaws against it for stability. I closed my eyes against the intense pain he would inflict as he tore my fingers off. But instead of biting, he licked. I opened my eyes to see his tongue flicking over my fingers, his googly eyes bright and excited, his tail wagging. Instinctively, I rubbed his nose. "Hey, boy," I said. He kept licking and pawed at the fence. I glanced at Cody. "Look," I said. "He's so friendly."

"Come on," Cody yelled.

But I couldn't kill that sweet dog. "No, Cody, come back. I'll keep him distracted, you go get the burger."

He swiveled his head toward me. "What?"

"I'll keep him distracted. Go get the burger."

He shook his head. "Bullshit," he said, still pushing through the brush. "Come on. We gotta get out of here."

That goofy-eyed dog suddenly quit licking, raised his nose in the direction of the rotten meat, and sniffed. He dropped to all fours. I scrambled toward the corner, but he sprinted past me. By the time I got there the collie had already scarfed half the meat and was working on the rest.

"Don't," I scolded him. "No!"

Finished, he looked up at me and licked his lips where a few bits of burger still clung.

"Come on," Cody yelled. He had exited the brush and was sprinting across the clearing.

I looked at that dog's two-colored eyes. "Oh, buddy," I said, "I'm so sorry."

Once we were well out of sight of the house, Cody turned to me. "Success," he said and held up his hand for a high-five. I walked past him without responding. He chattered all the way back, excited about our perfect plan and our victorious revenge.

At home, I told Mom I didn't feel too good and wanted to lie down. She agreed to take Cody home and told me not to budge from the house. Cody looked at me, disgusted, and shook his head. When Mom returned, she took my temperature.

"No fever," she said. "How are you feeling?"

"Not great."

"Well, you just rest."

I went out to the table when dinner was ready, but I only picked at the food without really eating. I said I'd like to go to bed early. Dad grunted. Mom nodded and then walked with me to my room. She kissed my forehead and wished me a good sleep.

I brushed my teeth, slipped off my jeans, and climbed into bed. My butt itched, and I knew I'd have a small scar there for the rest of my life. When I closed my eyes, I pictured that freshly turned dirt in our backyard, and I pictured Bo lying stiff and dead and rotting in his grave. Then I pictured that crazy-eyed dog lying in a similar grave stiff and dead and rotting, and how Needham would grieve his death just like I grieved Bo's. I cried myself to sleep.

Symmetry

Out of whack. Off-kilter. Unglued.

Whatever you want to call it, Beau knew how *broken* felt. And from the look of her, so did the massively pregnant Black Angus heifer eyeing him suspiciously from six feet away. He'd found her off by herself on the lee side of a low hill, struggling to give birth. The calf appeared to be hung up inside her. But he was trying to get close enough to see exactly what ailed her, if he could just put her at ease—to see whether the labor was actually dystocic, that is, or if she was just having a rough go her first time out.

"Besides my back, what ails me is my sister-in-law, mostly," he said in his soothingest voice, despite the bitter feelings about Tammy. "She moved into the house to nurse Wanda and me after our accident. But then she stayed."

As if in answer, the first-time mother made a low moaning noise, a sound of hurt and confusion mixed together.

"I hear you," he said softly, edging closer. "I can't claim to've suffered through labor, but I can sure enough relate. I've felt hurt and confused myself every day since the wreck."

He cleared her distended belly, near enough now to lightly touch her hip. Then he ran a gentle hand along her pin bone, working his way around until the calving situation came into view. Among the blood and amniotic fluid, partially obscured by her tail, Beau made out what looked to be a single hoof poking out of her birth canal—there should've been two hooves and a nose—and when she pressed back against him, desperate for relief from any quarter, he felt a contraction jolt through her. She was dystocic, all right. And the clock was ticking.

"Easy girl," he murmured. "We're gonna get that calf out of there."

But as was the case with his sister-in-law's hoped-for eviction, Beau wasn't sure yet how to make that happen. He'd dropped hints to Tammy during the early morning physical therapy sessions she'd been coaching him through, and he'd tried talking to Wanda about it last night in bed. But Tammy was either completely clueless or absolutely set on staying, or both. And Wanda's only response was to recite the Parable of the Good Samaritan from the Gospel of Luke, which meant the subject was closed. Instead of pushing, he'd flipped the TV onto a Spurs game on TNT.

Beau pulled out his pocket watch and timed the next contraction: a little over three minutes. She was deep into the delivery stage already. He looked around, weighing his options. In the near distance the rest of the gentle Black Angus cattle he'd added to the herd his father built speckled the winter-white coastal Bermuda of the 200-acre pasture. Farther away Beau made out some of the older brindle crossbred cows his father was so proud of—hardy and self-sufficient, at home in the brush—grazing near the barbed wire fence that divided the pasture from the tangled thicket that covered most of the 6000-acre Mulebach ranch. In addition to improving the herd with purebred stock in the years since his father passed, Beau had almost doubled the size of the spread. The cattle pens, with their headgate and the specially rigged maternity pen he'd set up for calf-pulling, stood a mile away on the far side of the brush. There was no way the heifer could walk it, and no time to fetch a trailer.

He turned and looked up at the house that he and Wanda had built atop the highest hill on the ranch and that they'd paid off with settlement money from the wreck. Even if he drove up there and called the vet, it would be the better part of an hour before Dr. Clayton arrived. By then the calf would be dead, if it wasn't dead already. Wanda wouldn't be home from her secretary job at the high school until the afternoon. And the thought of having Tammy help with the delivery was about the equivalent of cutting his ears off with a dull knife.

In the horse pasture next to the house, he saw the charcoal-dappled white coat of Lobo Blanco with his head down, grazing for all he was worth. The sight of the roping horse made Beau yearn to be out riding through the cattle again. He'd always been one to talk through the things that weighed heavy on his mind or his heart, and there was no better listener than Lobo Blanco—who in addition to being smooth-gaited and blessed with instinctive cow sense was smarter than a lot of the people Beau knew, including his sister-in-law. But despite months of intense physical therapy, the fused vertebrae at the base of his spine, the left hip that had been partially replaced, and the permanent pins in his left leg still made it impossible for Beau to ride a horse. On chilly winter mornings like this one, it was painful even to get behind the wheel of the pickup.

The heifer moaned again, bringing his attention back to the matter at hand. He was going to have to pull the calf himself, and it was going to have to happen right here. Right now. He opened the tailgate, removed the halter and ropes and buckets from the bed; then he took the dish soap, Vaseline, and disinfectant from behind the seat and nestled them into the dry grass beside the two buckets. Next, he gritted his teeth and hauled out the five-gallon water jug. As he awkwardly splashed water into both buckets, a flare of pain in the small of his back shot down into his left hip, sparking a fire that smoldered in his left thigh while he mixed disinfectant into the water in one bucket and sank one of the ropes into it.

"So much for the easy part," Beau said softly, picking up the halter and gently rubbing the soft black fur on the heifer's belly, then on her neck, easing his way toward her head. "This is where it gets interesting." He slipped the open halter over her nose, pulling the webbing up and tightening the buckle on the crownpiece in a single smooth motion before stepping back.

She shook her head and yanked on the lead rope, sending a blaze of pain down Beau's left side. But then another contraction hit, and all thought of the strange contraption on her head faded into the agony of trying to force out the stuck calf.

Beau wasted no time making the lead rope fast to the headache rack on the truck. Next, he cut a piece of twine from the ball in the glove box and tied the heifer's tail up across her back, looping the other end of the twine around her neck. As the contraction faded, he tilted his hat back and wiped off the sweat that had started on his forehead despite the sharp January air.

"Well? Are we good with this?"

The heifer stood calmly next to the truck, having apparently accepted both the halter and the tail-tie.

"Good girl." He shucked his jean jacket and rolled up his sleeves. "Now let's see what we've got."

He worked a dish-soap lather into a hand towel and scrubbed the heifer's hindquarters, rinsing off the bloody mess with the clean-water bucket. Then he washed and rinsed his hands and arms, shivering with the shock of the cold as he dipped them into the disinfectant, and mentally preparing myself for what was to come. The process of giving birth to something as big as a calf was all about symmetry. If the calf was properly aligned in the birth canal—in a forward presentation, a dorsal position, and a normal posture—as long as the cervix was sufficiently dilated, and the calf wasn't too big, both cow and calf generally came through just fine. In this particular case, something was out of whack. And there was only one way to set it right.

He lubed his hands and arms with Vaseline and then slathered the perineal area, carefully working his cupped fingers inside the birth canal. She wasn't fully dilated, that much was clear. And Beau still couldn't tell whether he had a front hoof—which he hoped was the case—or a back hoof. He started manually dilating the cervix as quick as he could without adding to the heifer's distress.

"At least it won't take rocket science to fix what ails you," he murmured through clenched teeth, the smoldering fire in his lower back flaring red-hot because of the awkward position he was in. "I've got a titanium ball for a hip joint, titanium pins holding my left femur together, and a fused lower spine. Try that sometime." Beau smiled a grim smile. "Better yet, try nine months of physical therapy with my sister-in-law."

Once the cervix was open, he worked his hands inside the uterus, pausing during the next contraction that tried to force his arms out with the stuck calf. He found another hoof, and felt the fetlock and knee bending in the same direction—which meant the calf was facing forward—and the angle of the bend told Beau the calf was definitely right side up.

"We've got a forward presentation and a dorsal position," he said softly, "so we're two-thirds of the way home. Once we get this calf out of you, you'll be on easy street. I'll still have a fitness-Nazi for a therapy coach, her two hyperactive boys bouncing off the walls of my house, and a Jesus junkie for a wife."

He didn't need the heifer to remind him that the *Jesus junkie* bit wasn't fair. Beau knew in his heart that Wanda had turned to religion in the aftermath of the wreck the same way he'd turned to watching sports on TV. She was as upset by what she called his *sports-habit* as he was by her being *born-again*. But the fact was that staring at athletes' bodies—powerful, graceful, pain-free—as they excelled on the television screen carried him back in time. In high school Beau had won the tie-down calf roping event at the Texas State Finals two years in a row, and he'd been winning roping matches and finishing in the money at rodeos across the Southwest ever since. Until his left side got crushed. The TV helped Beau remember what he was born to do and forget what the wreck was keeping him from. He wondered sometimes whether Wanda's churchgoing did that for her, too. But the honest truth was that he had no clue. After eleven years of symmetry, their marriage was as off-kilter as this heifer's parturition. And Beau had no idea how to set things straight again.

He couldn't seem to find the calf's head, which meant an abnormal posture. Instead of sharing this with the heifer, he pressed deeper with his right arm and finally felt an ear, then a mouth. And pushing his thumb past the calf's front teeth, Beau felt the mouth close around his finger and felt the tongue move in a suckle reflex.

"He's still alive! Or she is," he said, frankly surprised. "Although judging from the size of this bruiser's head, he's a bull. If I can just work his head up into a normal birthing posture, we may be able to get him out of you in time to keep him in the land of the living."

The heifer seemed to agree with every fiber of her being.

He pushed the exposed hoof back into the uterus, took a firm grip on the calf's muzzle, pulled it toward the opening in the pelvis. But before he could make sure whether the calf was properly aligned, another contraction started, and the first-time mother—so calm and so sensible up to now—panicked, shoving herself backwards and swinging her hind-quarters around to slam Beau against the truck. He felt a white flash of pain in his lower back as the door handle dug into his spine and felt his head smack hard against the door frame. Then his left hip seemed to explode. He tried to get his arms free, but the pressure from the uterine wall trapped them tight against the calf and he hung there, crushed between the heifer's shuddering body and the door until the contraction faded finally, and he was able to separate himself.

He slid down the side of the pickup, breathing heavy. From spine to knee his bones sizzled like they were made of molten metal. When his tailbone hit the ground, he felt the heifer step on his left leg. And suddenly, Beau was back inside the wreck. He felt again the shock of impact, the explosion of pain, the crushing weight that pushed the air out of his lungs as the big rig rolled over onto the Suburban. He remembered fighting to breathe. He heard Wanda's voice—high-pitched, panicked—pleading with God. Making promises. Telling Jesus that she wasn't ready, that Beau wasn't ready, that she'd do anything if God would just give them more time. "If you'll only keep us from dying, Jesus, I'll go to church twice every Sunday and on Wednesday night. I'll give up the whiskey drinking and the kinky sex. I'll bear witness to everyone I meet that you're the only thing on earth that matters." After two hours of agony on Beau's part and nonstop praying on hers, the Jaws of Life pried them out of that pancake of metal and flesh. And Wanda kept every promise.

Something cold and wet against his cheek brought Beau back to the pasture. The heifer nudged him again, and he managed to prop himself up against the door. He realized, vaguely, that he was missing his hat. He sat perfectly still, feeling fuzzy, the fire in his bones fading to a dull burn as he looked around for his Stetson. Beau silently cursed the heifer for her stupidity. He cursed the long-haul trucker who'd been at the wheel for seventeen hours without a break before plowing into the Suburban. He

111

cursed Wanda for focusing so completely on fulfilling her promises to Jesus that there wasn't room in her life for anything else. They hadn't made love since the wreck. He cursed Tammy for her piercing screech and drill-sergeant demeanor during therapy sessions—"Harder!" "Faster!" "Dig, dig, dig!"—and her need to take total control of everything in the house except her boys.

But mostly, Beau cursed himself. After all, this was the heifer's first calf. She hadn't known any better than to panic. He, on the other hand, knew from long experience that a dystocic cow's hormone levels were sometimes so wacky, and her pain so intense, she decided he was an enemy to vent her frustration on instead of a source of relief. Once again, Beau could relate. He'd certainly treated Tammy like an enemy, something he knew deep down to be unfair despite her coaching style and her takeover of what was supposed to be his castle. The reason Tammy had left her own home was to escape an abusive husband—a rancher named Needham she met and married while attending Howard Payne up in Brownwood, but who took to beating the living hell out of her and their young sons with increasing frequency and fervor. She filed for divorce not long after moving in with Wanda and Beau. Despite the negative impact on their marriage and on Beau's daily life, it was hard to blame Tammy for wanting to feel like she was in control for a change.

He felt the heifer's nose cold and wet against his cheek again, reminding him that he had things to do besides sit on the ground and feel sorry for himself. Hope for a live delivery was fading fast for her and her calf. In order for there to be any chance at all, Beau knew that the time had come to get to his feet. He started to haul myself up, only to feel an intense muscle spasm in his left hip. But just as he was mustering the resolve to make another effort, he caught the dull rumble of what could only be a vehicle approaching across the pasture.

Less than a minute later, Wanda rolled up. "Beau!" she yelled, stepping out of her brand-new black BMW Crossover and running over to where he sat. "Are you hurt?"

"I don't know," he said slowly, trying to figure out whether he was broken inside or just bruised. Despite all the Jesus business, and the possibility that he'd just crippled himself again, he felt his breath catch at the sight of his wife's stunning curves. "But I'm sure glad you're here."

"What happened?" she asked, kneeling beside him. "Why are you sitting on the ground?"

"A little while ago, I got caught in the middle of a wrestling match between this pregnant heifer and the truck. And right now I'm looking up at the best-looking woman in the county, who just happens to be my wife."

"You're scaring me. Did you hit your head? Your eyes look funny, and you're not acting like yourself."

"I was out for a minute, I think. And I seem to've lost my hat."

"I'm taking you to the hospital. Right now."

Beau shook his head, as much to clear the cobwebs as to respond to Wanda. "That unborn calf has minutes to live. And if I'm crippled again, I don't want it to've been for nothing. I was about to climb up the side of the truck and try to pull the calf myself, come what may."

"I'll run up to the house and get Tammy."

"There's no time. Now that you're here, we can do this together."

He looked up into Wanda's eyes, which he noticed for the first time in he didn't know how long were cornflower blue, and saw that they were full of tears. "But I've never done anything like this," she said. Then she glanced down at her skirt suit. "And I'm wearing Christian Dior."

"I guess the first thing to do, then, is take off your jacket and heels. After that, we'll get you washed up. We don't want to lose the heifer, whether we save the calf or not."

"The mother is in danger too?"

"When we pull the calf, we have to take it slow and easy, or we'll hurt her on the inside. Maybe bad enough to kill her. And if we don't keep everything sterile, and she gets an infection, she won't be a mother for long."

"Okay, what now?" Wanda asked, her teeth chattering as she stood wet from washing and in her stocking feet in the chill January air.

"The calf is coming frontwards and right-side up. His head was bent back, though, which is why he got hung up. I tried working it into a normal posture, but the heifer panicked and slung me against the truck. If I managed to get him aligned, our job will be easier. But I can't see the heifer's hindquarters from where I'm sitting. It would help if you could turn her around."

Wanda took the lead rope and swung the heifer 180 degrees about.

"That's better," Beau said, clearly making out two hooves this time instead of just one. "The hooves are perfectly presented. But I still can't make out the calf's nose. I'm afraid you're going to have to reach inside her."

"Oh Beau," Wanda said, dropping the lead rope. "No."

"You can do it. Just cup your hands and go right around the hooves. Then all you have to do is tell me what you feel inside the birth canal."

"I'm sorry." Turning her back on the heifer and on Beau, Wanda started toward the BMW. "I'll go get—"

"I'll make a deal with you," he called after her, his voice sounding every bit as ragged as he felt. "If you'll help me with this, and if the cow and calf both live, I'll give up TV."

Wanda stopped short and turned to face him. "Do you really mean that?"

"As God is my witness."

"He most certainly is," she said. Then she walked slowly and deliberately back. "Sweet Jesus, please help us to safely deliver this calf."

"Amen," Beau said. He didn't know whether it'd help any, but he guessed it couldn't hurt.

Wanda set her lips and reached inside the birth canal. "It's warm!" she said as if this fact surprised her. "And I think I feel a nose."

"Where?"

"Inside the heifer."

"I mean, where in relation to the hooves?"

"Right above them. And a little bit behind. But the calf still seems to be stuck."

"He's lined up all right. But he's too big for this first-time mother. We'll have to pull him. But first, we need to put the heifer down on her right side. He'll come through the pelvis easier that way, and it'll help her push."

"And how on earth am I supposed to throw a full-grown cow?"

"You're a natural," Beau said. "Just take that rope next to the disinfectant bucket and ease the end with the honda around her flank. Put the other end through the honda and pull it tight. Then all you have to do is pull the rope in the direction you want her to fall."

"It can't be that simple."

"Trust me. At this point, I'm surprised she's even able to stand."

Wanda clenched her jaw, picked up the rope, and threw the heifer. "I did it!" she said.

"All you need to do is trade that skirt suit and heels for jeans and boots, and you'll be ready to rodeo."

"Is that really what you want, Beau?" There was a timid tone in her voice now, a lost and searching sound that Beau hadn't heard in a long time.

114

It commanded his attention. He looked up at Wanda in her stocking feet with the rope clenched in her hands, her arms from fingertips to shoulders covered in blood and amniotic fluid. She'd never looked lovelier to him than at that moment. "What I really want," Beau said slowly, "is for things between us to be back like they were before the wreck."

"I want that too," she said, tears welling into her eyes again and mascara starting to streak her cheeks. "I left work early today, to try and reconnect with you. I brought a George Strait CD and Chuckwagon barbeque. I planned us a nice romantic date."

"It's chilly for a picnic," he said, feeling his own eyes start to sting. "The forecast called for sleet. But let's get this calf pulled, and if I haven't come completely unglued, we'll see what we can do. Okay?"

"Okay."

"To begin with, take that rope in the disinfectant bucket and tie it to the calf's front legs. Use both ends. Wrap the loops above each fetlock and take a half-hitch below the joint." While Wanda busied herself with the rope, Beau slid his way carefully around to the business end of the heifer. His back was sore. His left hip and leg ached. But he didn't feel any shooting pains, and everything seemed to be functioning. "The uterus is contracting down on the calf from all directions," he said, once the ropes were on tight and Wanda was sitting on the ground beside him, "so the best way to get him out of there intact is to pull first on one side, then on the other. We'll walk his shoulders out first, then we'll see about his hips."

"Should I start?"

"Go ahead. Brace your feet against the heifer's hindquarters and give a steady tug on the rope. She won't be going anywhere until we get that calf out."

Wanda set her feet and leaned back against the rope, getting leverage. "I can feel him moving!" she said as the calf's left fetlock slowly emerged. She almost fell over onto her back when the leg suddenly slipped out all the way to the knee.

"You did great!" Beau said quickly. "Just hold what you've got." He set his feet against the heifer's hindquarters and pulled on the rope, keeping the pressure steady until the right leg came through, along with the calf's head.

"There he is!"

"Part of him anyway," Beau said, guiding the calf's shoulders out of the birth canal. "And everything looks just like it's supposed to. Next, we'll rotate him so the widest part of his hips aligns with the widest part of the heifer's pelvis. This is usually where the mother takes a break. The umbilical cord is compressed, and while she's resting, the calf should start to breathe on his own."

"So what should we do?"

"Check the calf and wait. If his breathing is good, once we've rotated him, we might not have to do anything at all." Beau gently took the rope from Wanda's hands. "We might even have time for that picnic."

"I've been thinking all day about our first real date. You took me to the Chuckwagon for barbeque, remember? That's why I brought the take-out." She shifted her gaze from Beau's face down onto the calf's. "Then you took me parking out on your daddy's ranch."

Beau leaned forward and cupped a hand over the calf's nostrils. "Of course I remember," he said. "And it's our ranch now."

"You spread a blanket in the bed of your truck, wrapped your arms around me tight, and talked about the constellations and how the old-time cowboys used the Big Dipper to time their night watches on cattle drives. It's been a long time since you held me like that."

"Too long," Beau said. But he was thinking about what happened after the talking had ended, and the fireworks began. They'd spent the rest of the night making love in the bed of his truck. It had been a long time since they'd done that as well—and he was trying to find a way to say so, when he realized that he couldn't feel any breath coming out of the calf's nose. "Wanda, honey, do you have a pocket mirror in your car?"

"I've got a compact in my purse."

"I don't believe this calf is breathing. But I'll need a mirror to be sure."

Wanda was on her feet in an instant. And in less than a minute, Beau was holding a black fold-out makeup mirror under the calf's nose.

"If he's breathing at all," Beau said, "the mirror should fog."

"I don't see anything," Wanda half-whispered, half-sobbed. "We took too long. He's dead."

"Maybe not. I need you to take hold of his neck while I grab his front legs. When I give the word, twist him to the right with all you've got. We've got to rotate him forty-five degrees. Then we'll get back on the ropes and finish the delivery."

"I'm ready."

Beau took a deep breath, got to his knees, and wrapped his arms around the calf just below Wanda's arms. "Go!" he said, feeling the calf slowly swing around in the birth canal as the two of them applied torque and pressure. "That's got it! Now grab the rope and pull. Just like before."

Wanda plopped down beside him, braced her feet, and leaned back for leverage as they pulled on the rope together. To Beau's surprise, the calf fairly shot out of the birth canal, sending Wanda flat onto her back with the newborn in her lap.

"Are you okay?" Beau asked.

"Poor baby," Wanda said, hugging the calf against her. "Please don't be dead."

Beau reached past Wanda's arms and carefully cleared the mucus from the calf's nose and throat. "Now I need you to rub him. Hard. Like you're trying to scour off his fur. That should stimulate him to breathe."

Wanda dug her fingers into the calf's soaking-wet coat and started working them back and forth. "Like this?"

"Perfect. Keep it going. I'll be right back." He limped around to the passenger side of the pickup, his body feeling bruised but not broken, and took a foot-long piece of garden hose out of the glove box. When he got back to Wanda, he held the mirror up to calf's nostrils again. "Still nothing."

"Oh no," Wanda moaned. "Oh no."

"We're going to have to try artificial respiration. I need you to stop rubbing so I can get this into his nose." Beau worked one end of the tube into a nostril, then straightened the length of hose and knelt beside the calf. "When I tell you, cup one hand around his muzzle, and with the other plug the open nostril while I blow. Ready, go!" He breathed into the hose, watching the calf's chest slowly expand as his lungs filled with air, then Beau removed the hose to let the air flow out. He breathed into the calf again. And again. Until finally the newborn kicked, threw his head back, and started breathing on his own.

"He's alive!" Wanda shouted, startling the new mother and Beau. "He's alive! We did it!"

"Shh ... It was you who did most of it," Beau said, his voice a hoarse whisper. "And I'm proud of you and our teamwork. But now we need to back off so that this new mother and her calf can bond. It looks like they're both going to be okay."

"Do you think it would hurt anything if I washed up first?"

He looked at Wanda, then down at himself. They were both as wet as the newborn calf. "I'll join you," Beau said.

They cleaned off as best they could. Then he wrapped his jean jacket around her shoulders and they climbed into the truck. Beau turned the heater on full blast, and as their shivering slowly subsided, they watched the new mother get up and start licking her calf.

"It's beautiful," Wanda said.

"It is," Beau said. "But it's not over quite yet. We've got to wait and see whether he's strong enough to get up and suckle. That was a rough delivery, so it may take a couple of hours."

"Will she keep licking him until he nurses?"

"Yes. I guess we've got time for that picnic now. Although, truth be told, I don't feel much like eating barbeque."

"I don't feel much like eating barbeque either," Wanda said, still staring at the calf. "We could listen to George Strait. I've got his greatest hits CD in the car."

Beau reached over and took Wanda's hand that still felt chilly. "You asked me earlier if I remembered our first date. The place I took you parking that night, the place where we were completely together for the first time, was at the top of the highest hill on the ranch." He gestured with the hand holding Wanda's up at the house they'd built. "Why do you think I picked that as the site for our new home?"

"I guess I knew that, but it sounds good to hear you say it. And I'm ready to be with you in that way again. But it seems like all you've done since the accident is watch TV."

"I made you a promise about that today," Beau said. "A promise I aim to keep. But it seems to me like all you've done since the wreck is go to church, read the Bible, and pray."

"Those are not things I'm willing to give up," Wanda said, but she squeezed his hand as she said it. "And maybe you don't have to completely give up TV either. We just have to make a space for ourselves in between."

"How are we going to make a space for ourselves if our house is full of Tammy and those boys?"

"You're forgetting the Parable of the Good Samaritan."

"Am I?" Beau took a deep breath, held it, then let it out again. "Seems like I remember the Good Samaritan taking that robbery victim to an inn and paying his room and board. Maybe we could do something like that for Tammy."

"You mean help her find a place of her own?"

He nodded, cautiously hopeful for the first time since the wreck. "We could pay her rent until she finds a job."

"She and those boys are the only family I've got besides you." The timid, searching tone that had shaken Wanda's voice earlier was long gone. "We'll have to see how Tammy feels about it first. And if she says no, she stays."

"If that's the cost of getting you and me moving in the right direction again, so be it. I'll abide by her decision. And yours. But I think birthing that calf proves I don't need a fitness coach anymore."

"Oh Beau, look!" Wanda said. "Look!"

Through the tiny flakes of sleet that had started to fall on the windshield, he saw the calf heave shakily to his feet and start nursing while the new mother nudged his hindquarters in encouragement. "Our job here is done," Beau said. "Shall we head on up to the house and have that talk with Tammy?"

Wanda slid across the seat and leaned into him, her body pressing seamlessly against his right side, the side that had never been broken. The sleet glittered on the windshield like stars. "Let's stay and watch a while," she said.

Baby Head

James McKneely parked his Jeep beside Highway 16 and looked across the field of hardscrabble and mesquite at the old cemetery. Someone had erected a new barbed wire fence close to the gravestones. "Baby Head is the place where important things begin," his mother had told him more than once. But she never told him what things, only that he would know "someday."

A few days before, he had learned part of the story, and he figured this was the day when he learned the rest.

He got out of the Jeep, took off his heavy policeman's uniform shirt and put on his safety vest. Central Texas January air rippled his skin, but he was glad for the cool because the vest in summer months made him too warm.

With his shirt on again and tucked neatly into his trousers, he tapped his pocket to make sure he had the letter the lawyer had given him, and he strapped on his utility belt. He put on his policeman's hat before crossing the field to the fence.

A live oak, stressed and yellowing from the drought, had managed to drop some acorns on the ground close to the new fence. A few scruffy mesquites dotted the landscape, most looking dead, and the cactus wore the maroon hue typical of prickly pears near death from lack of water. Not very promising of new beginnings of any kind, James thought, though he knew the desert plants were alive enough and would declare themselves green again come warmer weather and some rain. A sprinkle would do. But right then, the whole area struck him as dead as the stones scattered across the hardscrabble, dead as those beneath the grave markers.

His mother, reaching to him from beyond her grave in Amarillo and doing so with a letter written when she was barely still alive, directed his next steps: go into Baby Head and find the tomb of Jodie May McKneely. An ancestor, his mother might have told him; but if she had, she would have been lying. Baby Head cemetery was old and long abandoned, the people buried there mostly forgotten with some few remembered only in gossip, legends of violence, and stories of meanness and suffering.

The name *McKneely* never had felt right to him, and he knew why. Once, when he was so young that he could barely remember, he had been James Needham, but that name somehow slipped away, and he became James McKneely. It was a name change his mother steadfastly refused to explain until she was near death, and even then she gave the information only in a bizarre letter.

A glance at his watch told him that Laverne wasn't due to arrive for another ten minutes. She would park close to his Jeep exactly upon her assigned hour. James felt certain of that, for she had been punctual all her life. Their dangerous brother would not be far behind.

Ralphie. James chuckled at the silliness of his brother for sticking with his childhood name. "Maybe," James once told Laverne, "he figures that someone with an innocent-sounding name couldn't possibly be an acid-head, a drunk, a needle freak, or a thief."

"He's much more than that," Laverne said, though her tone had not conveyed any real belief.

Holding down a strand of barbed wire with one hand, James squeezed through the fence with only a tiny tug of one barb nicking the back of his shirt. Just as he located the tombstone of Jodie May McKneely, he saw Laverne's car pull off the highway and stop behind his Jeep. His impulse was to help her through the fence. But he knew better, for Laverne would bristle at any offer of help. He watched her take a basket and what appeared to be a blanket from her car. Leave it to my sister, James thought, to make a business meeting into a picnic.

He watched Laverne try to shake her sweater loose from one of the fence barbs, and he heard a small tear of cloth.

As she bestowed a formal hug on her older brother, she said, "James."

"Laverne." James endured the hug. "You brought lunch?"

"Refreshments. No telling how long it'll take for us to share Mom's letters and to discuss whatever is in them."

James pointed at the tombstone. "Jodie May McKneely was a child, not an ancestor."

"I read about her and about this cemetery on the web. Jodie was a few months shy of her third birthday. I don't know how we are related to her."

"We're not." James pulled an envelope from his back pocket. "Maybe Mom will explain more in one of her letters."

"Ralphie." Laverne pointed.

James and Laverne watched Ralph McKneely park his rent-a-wreck and get out of the car. "No rifle," Laverne said. "But he never liked rifles. He'll be packing."

"Maybe. If so, it'll be a sneaky little Saturday night special, a cheap excuse for a pistol and dangerous mainly to him."

"Don't count on that. He told me he has plans for you, and he said it with a mean sneer in his voice. He intends you harm. Did you wear your Argyle city police outfit to try to scare him?"

"Nope. The list of instructions the lawyer gave me said Mom requested I come in my blues. She also said you and Ralphie have letters to read here beside Jodie May's tombstone."

"I got the same instructions about letters from the lawyer in Amarillo when he gave me my letter from Mom. I'm to read it to you boys. Mom always was a control freak."

"Hey, Sis," Ralph called from the fence. "Hey, asshole cop."

"You're in for some real trouble," Laverne whispered to James. She turned toward her other brother. "Hello, Ralphie."

Ralph slipped through the fence without a snag.

"Hey, slick," James said. My rogue brother, he thought, looks as unkempt as ever with his scraggly beard, black hoodie, dirty jeans, and scuffed-up boots.

"Lookit you," Ralph said. "Decked out like a hot-shot Argyle cop. But this ain't even close to Argyle, and you got no jurisdiction here."

"Mom told him to wear his uniform to our meeting," Laverne said.

"And if she told me to wear a tuxedo, do you think I'd show up dressed as a good little penguin?"

"I suppose it's good to see you, too," James said. "We were talking about those letters we're supposed to read to each other. Did you bring yours?"

"Why should I tote Mom's manipulative letter across the state? Did she really think that I care if she cut me out of her will for being a bad boy and disobeying her last command? You keep her inheritance, all twenty-eight cents of it."

"You don't know?" Laverne asked.

"She left a bit more than twenty-eight cents," James said.

"Sure she did. Maybe thirty cents."

"The three of us," James said, "are supposed to divide three hundred thousand dollars. And some change—maybe twenty-eight cents—but only if we follow her instructions."

"You're a lying sumbitch," Ralph said. He pointed at the tombstone. "That McKneely died when she was three. I thought we was supposed to meet at the tomb of an ancestor."

123

"We don't know why Rose had us meet here," Laverne said. "And Mom did leave that much money. She invested Keith's money after he died, and she never told us about it."

"You know her rules about the letters," James said. "Read her letter to us here. Looks like you pulled one of your usual tricks, and this time you shot yourself in the foot. No letter to share in Baby Head, no inheritance."

"Ease up on him," Laverne said.

"Keith didn't up and die without help," Ralph said. "You murdered him, big brother, mister high-and-mighty. You and Mom put me in the psycho slammer when it was you they should have locked away years ago. Hell, you should have got the needle, you murdering bastard. The only good thing Mom ever did for me was to send me that letter from the grave telling me how you killed Keith, and he was your very own step-daddy, and a good man, and you murdered him."

"You were only two when Keith had his final heart attack," James said, "and I was four. Also, Keith was far from being a good man."

"Heart attack, my ass." Ralph squatted, pulled a knife from a boot, stood, and lurched at James.

James stumbled, steadied himself, grabbed Ralph's wrist and twisted. The knife clattered against Jodie May's tombstone. James twisted again, jerking Ralph to his knees.

"You're breaking my wrist," Ralph said.

"Did he stab you?" Laverne asked. She had snatched up what James figured was part of a tree limb fallen from one of the mesquites, and she held it like a baseball player would hold a bat.

"He sure as hell tried." James pushed Ralph down, pinned him with a knee, and handcuffed him. He glanced at Laverne. "I like your weapon, though it's bound to have some mesquite thorns on it."

Laverne tossed aside the club. "I thought he had stabbed you. In the heart."

"Close." James zip-tied Ralph's ankles together, did a fast frisk, and pulled a small pistol from one of his pockets. In a few efficient moves James took the shells out of the pistol and set it on the top of Jodie May McKneely's tombstone.

"I thought he would be packing," Laverne said.

"That's for snakes," Ralph said. "There's tons of snakes in old cemeteries like this."

"You would tell a lie," James said, "when the truth sounded better." He sat Ralph up and leaned him against the gravestone. "You miserable excuse for a brother." James put a finger into a hole in his shirt. "You ruined my best shirt."

"That cut in your shirt is right over your heart." Laverne stepped closer to James, her face showing alarm.

"Vest," James said. "Kevlar. I'll have a bruise, though the vest has some good padding in it. You picked up that mesquite club like I once picked up a baseball bat. Nice."

"Do you suppose," Laverne asked, "that Rose knew wearing your uniform also meant you would be wearing a Kevlar vest?"

"So Mom guessed that Ralph would try to stab or shoot me. Amazing." James looked with contempt at Ralph. "You finally made a real attempt to kill me. But I forgive you."

"I forbid you to forgive me," Ralph said. "You murdering hypocrite."

"Too late." James was aware that the smile he showed Ralph was too toothy and neither genuine nor kind.

"Cut the zip-tie off my legs," Ralph said. "Get these cuffs off. I have Rose's letter to read to you. She said in the letter that you're a killer."

"You don't have Mom's letter," Laverne said.

"Memorized. I got it memorized. If I tell what Rose said in the letter, will you set me free?"

"No," James said, and at the same time Laverne said, "Yes."

"So which is it, yes or no?" Ralph demanded.

"Tell us and I'll decide," James said.

"Then it will be a no. But what the hell, here goes. Mom said that when you was four, you murdered Keith. Our very own step-father, and a nice guy who didn't deserve what you did."

"A four-year-old murderer?" Laverne laughed. "Even you can make up a better story than that. Keith Dutt died of a heart attack."

"Mom wrote in her letter to me," Ralph said, "that James thought Keith was beating her, so mister innocent little James went to his room for his baseball bat. He whacked Keith across the shins, and that made him fall to his knees, then James got him whack! right in the back of the head with the bat. Killed him dead as a mackerel."

"I didn't just think Keith was beating Rose. I knew it, saw him doing it. Bloodied her nose, knocked out one of her teeth. I remember that day better than I want to. It was the blood gushing from her nose and across her mouth that sent me after the bat. Rose called an ambulance after I hit Keith. He had a bad heart, and a heart attack got him, maybe because of all the excitement over beating Mom."

"I know the story," Laverne said. "Mom told it to me many times. It was a heart attack that killed Keith, and he was abusing her. She liked to tell how Keith talked to the medics in the ambulance on the way to the hospital."

"On her deathbed," Ralph said, "Rose told the story in her letter to me—with one important difference. Keith did talk to the ambulance boys, then passed out, then died of a brain bleed from the damage James did with that bat. He was a goner when they got to the hospital."

"I don't believe Rose wrote all that," James said.

"It's in the letter in her own handwriting. I still have it somewhere."

"Maybe," James said. "I could believe a four-year-old did some real damage with the bat."

"Not just any four-year-old," Ralph said. "You. You killed him. And now look at you, mister high-and-mighty Argyle cop."

"So that's why you tried to stab your brother?" Laverne asked. "Because you think he killed Keith Dutt?"

"You know better than that," Ralph said. "James set up that so-called intervention that got me locked up in the loony slammer they call the Pavilion up in Amarillo."

"I went to that intervention, too," Laverne said. "So why not stab me? And Mom was there. And three of your friends and your ex-wife and two of your ex-bosses. You were killing yourself with your drinking, and you needed help. Or did you forget?"

"James did it," Ralph said. "He did that to me. Not the rest of you."

"You were drunk for three months," James said. "Your wife left you. You wrecked your pickup, lost your job, and you let your dog run loose, so it got run over." James turned to Laverne. "He became a country-and-western drinking song. I thought he'd hit rock bottom, that it was time for an intervention."

"See?" Ralph said. "See? James did it. Then he and Rose had me committed for months. Months! So yeah, I wanted to get a piece of him with my boot knife, and after reading Mom's letter about him being a murderer, who could blame me for going after a killer—worse, a cop who is a killer."

"I'm so sad for you, Ralphie," Laverne said. "But I don't believe Rose said any of that in her letter to you."

"She sure as hell did."

"I suppose it is possible," James said. "But we need to share Mom's other letters here in this weird little cemetery. Shall I start with a letter she wanted me to read?" He held up an envelope.

"You said you would take the cuffs off if I told. You said. You said."

"I most certainly did not say that. But okay, I'll free up your legs." He cut the zip-tie from Ralph's ankles. "Do something else stupid, and I'll hog-tie you and toss you into the trunk of that wreck of a car you parked over there."

"The cuffs. The cuffs." Ralph held out his arms.

"You bring a knife to stab me and a pistol to shoot me, and now that you failed to do either, you expect me to free your hands?"

"I have a blanket here that we can sit on while we read the letters," Laverne said. "And some hot tea and some chicken salad sandwiches." She spread the blanket close to Jodie May McKneely's gravestone.

"I'll stand for now," James said.

Ralph sat on a corner of the blanket, rubbed his ankles, glared at James, and with movements made awkward from the handcuffs, accepted a sandwich and a mug of tea.

"This letter," James said, "is in two parts, the first part she wrote in black ink and in tight, controlled handwriting. The second part is scraggly and barely controlled and written with a blue ball point that was running out of ink. Both are long, so I'll do some summarizing."

"Read it," Ralph said. "I don't trust you to tell it all."

"That's a joke, right?" Laverne said.

James held the letter up. "I'll make copies later for both of you. Rose starts with names. She says the name on this tombstone became ours, says we might have wondered why our aunt Wanda and Uncle Beau Mulebach sometimes call Rose *Tammy*. I'll admit that I wondered about that. Rose says her parents named her Tammy, that she became Tammy Needham when she got married. Says here that he was a terrible man whose only good deed in his entire life was to father Ralphie and me. The letter says that Needham abused Mom, and he took to striking me and Ralphie until one day without any planning she put her boys in her car and left."

"What about Keith?" Ralph asked. "I thought she married Keith."

"Rose never married Keith," Laverne said.

"I'll get to that," James said. He scanned the letter while he spoke. "That same day, driving away from Needham's house, she saw the sign on Highway 16 pointing to Baby Head Cemetery, and in her woo-woo way she somehow knew the cemetery called out to her, so she drove in, took Ralphie and me among the graves to look around. She was feeling so high on her new freedom and so happy to be away from Needham that when she saw this grave marker, she knew in a flash that her family's name should be McKneely. Poor little Jodie May McKneely, Mom says in her letter, never got to live her life because death took her at such an early age, so it had to be fate that took Rose and her boys into the cemetery."

"Damn," Ralph said. "But it was Mom and her silly letters that brought the three of us into Baby Head today. Not fate."

"I doubt fate had anything to do with any of this," James said.

"Maybe," Laverne said, "fate did lead her here."

"Let me finish," James said. He returned to scanning the letter. "Mom thought the name was proper for her and her boys because she so hated Needham. Says here that she also peeled away her own first name. That's a quote: 'peeled away the name *Tammy*.' And this is a part that much astonished me. She wrote that since her liberty rose for the first time that day, she took it for her name from then on. Liberty Rose McKneely."

"I'll be damned," Ralph said.

"I had not known that she believed her first name became *Liberty*," James said.

"I knew that was her name," Laverne said, "but until now, I didn't know how she got the name."

"Why didn't she tell me and Ralphie?" James asked.

"I think Rose told me more of her secrets than she did you boys," Laverne said.

"That's about it for the first part of her letter," James said. "Oh, yeah. She also said she taught her boys and later Laverne to call her Rose or Mom, whichever we preferred."

"Mom was nuts," Ralph said. "And we're nuts to be meeting here— to be doing anything she tells us to do in her screwy letters."

"The next part," James said, "must be something Rose wrote later, the messy part in blue ink. Here she crabs about our family having too many secrets."

"All families have secrets," Laverne said.

"Maybe," Ralph said. "But if anyone gave prizes for the most secrets, we McKneelys would get the blue ribbon. That is, if *McKneely* is really our name."

"It is our name," Laverne said, "though maybe it shouldn't be."

"In this part of her letter," James said, "Mom admits that she is the cause of all the family secrets, and she says she feels bad about that. Then she goes on to talk about Keith Dutt. She met him not long after her brief stop in Baby Head Cemetery. She thought he was wonderful until he began his abuse, which at first was only verbal, and Rose ignored it mainly because she was soon pregnant and because she met Sarah Laverne who became her good friend and confidant. It was, Mom says, a friendship that changed her life in good ways. And we know most of the story about her friend—the breast cancer, Sarah's terrible death."

"Yeah, yeah," Ralph said. "That's a story Rose told us plenty of times. So is that it? There's nothing else in the letter?"

"Be patient, Ralphie," Laverne said.

"There's more," James said. "Another secret, Mom's big secret, and this one is a whopper. It seems that on her deathbed, Sarah Laverne told Rose that Sarah would return to life as Rose's child, and that Rose should name her *Laverne*. Sarah said to watch the child with care to see the basic personality of Sarah emerge as Laverne grew up."

"This is a disturbing secret," Laverne said. "Rose should have told me."

"Mom addresses that issue," James said. "She writes that she had never believed in reincarnation until she watched so much that was Sarah being acted out by Laverne."

"I don't believe this tripe," Ralph said.

"Hush, Ralphie," Laverne said. "Go on, James."

"I guess it's no big surprise," James said, "that Mom would come to believe what Sarah told her about coming back as Mom's McKneely baby. With her growing belief, Rose worried about the issue of telling Laverne. Rose compares telling Laverne about her past life to telling adopted children about their biological parents. She thinks adopted children have a right to know about their other parents and wonders if she should tell her daughter so she could better understand herself. I'll read two sentences of the letter. 'If I shared that information with my daughter, would the knowledge harm her or help her? I didn't know, so I kept the secret, and now I think doing so was wrong.' There's one other thing in Mom's letter, but we need to hear from Laverne before I share that."

"Tell us now," Laverne said.

"You read your letter from Mom first."

"Wow," Ralph said. "Rose was more of a nut case than I thought, and I knew she was plenty nutty. Are you okay with all this weird reincarnation stuff, Laverne?"

"That information explains much that I have wondered about," Laverne said.

"It explains about Rose," James said, "not about you." He sat beside his sister on the blanket. "Are you okay?"

"Rose was some kind of mystic," Ralph said, "something we all knew, but she was more far-out in her beliefs than we imagined. Are you okay, Laverne?"

"Are you?" James asked.

"Would you boys stop it? Yes, I'm okay. Better than okay. There might be some comfort in the possibility that I have the soul of Rose's best friend."

"But it's not true," Ralph said. "You don't have a soul, certainly not someone else's. You are a soul."

James stared at his brother in surprise.

"Ralphie is right about Rose," Laverne said. "She was much weirder than any of us knew, and I for one imagined her to be plenty weird."

"People," Ralph said, "are not as strange as you imagine. They are stranger than you can imagine."

"That's twice today," James said to Ralph, "that you have amazed me in good ways."

"It's my turn to tell about a letter from Rose, right?" Laverne took an envelope from her purse.

"There's no way Rose can top that last secret," James said, "though it's just a screwy idea and not a real secret at all."

"Maybe not," Laverne said. She opened her letter and scanned the first page. "I'll do this like James did and give you a summary. She starts by saying it is high time we stopped using Ralph's baby name, *Ralphie*. Ralph, she proclaims here, is the only person she knows about in her family who has an addictive personality, so he did not inherit his addictions. She says she did some genealogical research on that issue. Here is Mom's big secret concerning Ralphie—uh, Ralph. She concludes that his abuse of alcohol and drugs was burned into him during her pregnancy."

"Bull," Ralph said. "You're making this up."

"I wish I were," Laverne said. "She says your being a substance abuser is her fault because she smoked and drank wine when she was pregnant with you. She said when you moved about in her womb, you sometimes stretched out, so she could feel where your head and feet were on different sides of her."

"Mom told me about that," James said.

"Yeah," Ralph said. "I've heard that from her."

"But there's more," Laverne said. "Rose says that when Ralph stretched out like that, it hurt her. She also says that she noticed the fetus did that only when she smoked or drank, so the cigarettes and wine had to be hurting Ralphie. It took her a while to realize she was inflicting pain on her baby, but when she finally understood and stopped the smoking and drinking, it was too late, for the damage, she believed, was done, though she didn't know it for sure until Ralph was a teenager and began smoking pot, then went to alcohol, then to LSD, then to—"

"Yeah, yeah, yeah," Ralph said. "We all know what I did, so no need to harp on it."

"Rose's real secret here isn't about you, Ralph. It's about her. She thought she was to blame for your bad behavior. But she does lecture you in this letter. She tells you that while she harmed you years ago, you need to get over it and be your own person. 'Grow up,' she says. And that's a quote. 'Grow up and stop hurting yourself.' She asks you to forgive her, and she says she forgives you for all your drinking and drug abuse." Laverne's voice broke, and she blinked repeatedly. "Here is her final statement, which she wrote in capital letters, 'I forgive you, and now please, please forgive me.'"

"That's powerful," James said.

"Wow," Ralph said. "I never knew I made Mom feel guilty." He cleared his throat and seemed on the verge of tears. "I wish I could tell her," his voice trailed off, "tell her ..."

"In Rose's letter to you, Ralph," James asked, "did she really make the claim that I murdered Keith Dutt?"

Ralph sat in silence, staring at the handcuffs.

"This is a good time to share Mom's other request of us," James said. "And this just might be the real reason Rose made us meet here in this odd place. But first." He stood and approached Ralph. "Hold out those cuffs."

James could see the surprise on Ralph's face, watched him nod as in understanding and hold out his arms.

James set the cuffs on the top of Jodie May's tombstone beside the pistol. He unfolded the letter again. "Here is a direct quote from Rose. It's in that shaky handwriting I mentioned, and it might be the last thing she ever wrote. '*McKneely* is not your proper last name, even if I hired a lawyer to make it your legal name. That terrible name *Needham* isn't proper in this family, either, nor is *Dutt* right for Laverne, even if Keith Dutt was her father. I want the three of you to choose a new last name like I once chose my entire name, Liberty Rose McKneely. I hope you can do it together, and that you will not choose a dead name from a tombstone as I did. It was a mistake, and that name cursed us all.'"

James folded the letter. "And that, I promise, is the end of her letter."

"Damn," Ralph said.

"I didn't see that coming," Laverne said.

"We don't have to rename ourselves," James said, "though you gotta admit that it is a rather good idea."

"It's a weird idea," Laverne said, "though it sounds worth considering."

"Strange," Ralph said. "Damned strange. But it is what Mom wanted."

"We've been given a huge question," James said. "If you suddenly discover that your name doesn't fit you, what new name would you choose? Sometime soon, but not today and not in a cemetery, the three of us need to discuss how to find the right name."

James thought he saw a kind of agreement in the faces of his sister and brother.

Good Fences

A little after two a.m., less than a mile from home and despite the thermos of coffee I had poured down my throat, I lost control of my eyelids and they drifted shut for a few seconds. When my chin hit my chest, I jerked awake just in time to crank the wheel away from the embankment my truck targeted. The old Dodge fishtailed and spun me toward the other side of the county road, down a gentle two-foot slope and through a barbed wire fence. I bumped to a stop maybe thirty yards inside the fence line.

"Shit!" I yelled and stomped my feet against the floorboard. I knew I should have waited to head home. But it was the Friday starting Spring Break my senior year at Angelo State, and I had been eager to leave exams and papers and any reminders of them behind for a while.

I had pulled the short straw at work and had to tend bar at Graham Central Station that Friday night while most of my cohorts headed to places far more fun. My shift lasted until two, but because business was slow I'd sweet-talked my manager into letting me leave by midnight. And I'd headed for home and an intimate meeting with that damned fence.

I took a minute to breathe deeply and shake off the shock of the accident, then cranked the wheel and banged my truck back onto the caliche road. I stopped to assess the situation. I had taken out several T-posts, but my one bit of good luck was that the main posts were intact. The really bad luck was that I had just driven through old man Needham's fence. I'd never forgiven him for killing my dog Bo when I was twelve, nor had I forgiven myself for killing his rangy border collie out of a twelve-year-old's sense of justice. I'd had a few run-ins with him over the next ten years, but like most people in the county I avoided him as much as possible. He was known as a mean old bastard, but unlike most independent ranchers, he was rich—and thus influential, and he could get away with more than most folks. What he got away with was never friendly.

If it had been up to me, I'd have taken out his entire fence. Still, having grown up in a ranching family, I knew you could never be responsible for another man's cattle getting out, no matter what you thought of that man. I allowed myself another spate of cursing, then shoved my door open and dug through my cross-bed tool box for three ratchet straps. I strung the straps between posts to block the gap my truck had opened, checked that they were tight and wouldn't slip, and drove to the home place.

My folks had gone to bed long before but roused enough to welcome me home before I fell into bed fully clothed and slept the proverbial sleep of the dead. When I arose at six and stumbled to the kitchen, my dad greeted me with a strong cup of coffee, fried bacon, scrambled eggs, and biscuits. "Thanks," I said, then took a chair and dug in.

"I'd help," Dad said, "but your mom's got an eye appointment." I nodded, my mouth stuffed with eggs scrambled in bacon grease. Every bite was a little haven of comfort. "She doesn't like to drive with her eyes dilated."

I wiped my mouth on a paper napkin. "No problem. Shouldn't take me long."

"Roll of barbed wire in the barn," he said and paused to sip his coffee. "Take whatever else you need."

I filled my thermos with more coffee and drove down to the barn, where I loaded a roll of wire, the stretcher, some splicing sleeves, T-posts, and the post driver. My hope was to repair Needham's fence and be out of sight before he knew what had happened.

I arrived just as a sliver of sun bulged above the horizon. By the time I double-checked the damage to determine what work lay ahead of me, unloaded tools, and released the ratchet straps, I had plenty of light to begin work. My truck had uprooted two T-posts and bent two more. I dug the bent ones out and began replacing all four. My luck was holding; I'd seen no sign of old man Needham. The morning was bright and mild, but after driving the new posts sweat stained my shirt. Still, I didn't take a breather, eager as I was to get it done and get gone.

The splicing went smoothly, but as I finished the last of four strands—the top one—I saw dust billowing just down the county road. I grabbed the wire stretcher and headed for my truck. Needham eased his Ford to within a couple inches of my tailgate so I had no access from there. I hefted the stretcher over the side and dropped it in, then turned and went back for the spool of wire.

"Well son of a bitch." Needham had stepped out of his truck and leaned on the hood. "Trespassing again." Ten years before, my lab pup Bo had chased a jackrabbit onto Needham's place, and I rolled under the fence and tore after him. That was the first trespassing offense Needham chalked up against me. He had gotten to Bo before I did and shot him with a .22 rifle. Then, when I struggled to lift Bo and get out of there, the old man went after my butt with a pellet gun. Two weeks later, I poisoned his border collie, and for a month afterwards I cried myself to sleep thinking about what I'd done.

There by the patch job I'd just finished, I looked over my shoulder at his fence and then down at the ground where I stood. "Don't believe I'm on your property."

"Looks like you damn sure have been." He nodded toward my tire tracks from the night before.

"No longer than it took me to turn around and get the hell out."

"Trespassing's trespassing, boy."

I lugged the spool to my truck bed and dropped it in.

He pulled a flask from his back pocket and took a swig. In recent years, he'd become a hard-core alcoholic. Dad had told me about finding him in one or another drunken predicament over the last few years. Once, Dad spotted Needham's truck wedged between two boulders in a dry creek bed. The old man sat in the truck, bottle of Jack Daniels in hand, apparently oblivious to his dilemma. Headed to the feed store early one morning, Dad had also seen the old geezer's truck parked in front of his gate, him slumped over the steering wheel. Dad checked to see if he was dead, but Needham roused and mumbled something about dropping his key in the dark. Then he cussed Dad for waking him up.

"You ain't done," Needham said to me as I rounded my truck toward the driver's-side door. "Wire's too loose."

I walked back to the fence, grabbed the top strand with both gloved hands, and leaned back with all my weight. It gave a little, as it should, but it didn't snap, and it didn't sag when I released it. I shook my head. "Looks perfect to me."

"Listen, you little shit, I'm done with your trespassing and lawbreaking. I'll be calling the sheriff."

I slipped my cell from my jeans pocket and snapped three pictures of the repaired fence. He had money, and money meant influence, but even money couldn't buy the law. "Go ahead. Call him." I held my phone out in his direction.

"You bet your ass I will. But not on your little Japanese gadget there." He took another pull from the flask and glared. Then he spat in the dirt and climbed back into his truck. As he drove past, he raised a middle finger in my direction. The old bastard.

Back at home, I told Dad about my run-in with Needham. He cursed the old man. "Should have shot him the last time he accused us of trespassing."

That had been one September four years after Needham killed Bo. Dad and I were out on horseback checking the cattle when we spotted a deer hung in the fence that bordered Needham's place and ours. Both back legs were twisted bad in the top strands of barbed wire. The legs were broken. The merciful thing was to put it out of its misery, but we'd brought only a shotgun with bird shot in case we saw doves. Dad sent me back to the house to fetch his .223 rifle. Riding to the house, locating the rifle and bullets, and riding back took a good thirty minutes. In the meantime, to ease the doe's pain, Dad had used his wire cutters to release it from the pressure of the barbs. He assumed it wouldn't be able to move and so would be there when I returned. But the poor thing had struggled, lunging and falling, until it was twenty yards or so away. It lay behind a cedar, panting and defeated. The low-growing branches blocked any possibility of shooting the poor creature.

We knew she could lie there for several days until finally dying from lack of water and food. The best thing was to shoot her—a quick and sudden death that would spare her the slow painful one she faced from dehydration and starvation. With the top two strands of wire cut, we could easily hike legs over the fence. When we rounded the cedar, we heard the growl of a truck engine somewhere nearby. Dad reacted quickly, raised the rifle, and shot the deer in the head. Then we hurried back toward the cut fence. We scrambled over just before Needham's truck appeared. He simply scowled at us, gunned the engine, and drove away. That, in his mind, had been the second trespassing offense—or maybe the third, since I had been on his place when I poisoned his dog.

The sheriff arrived a couple hours after Dad and I had returned to the house. He listened to our story and said, "Okay, but for God's sake, stay off that asshole's property."

And he showed up again the day after I patched the old man's fence where I had driven through it. "I'm sorry," he said. "I have to follow up on complaints."

I nodded. "No problem." I talked. He listened. He nodded.

"Just try to lay low for the rest of your break."

"Count on it."

For the next few days, I stayed put on our place. Dad and I tended to cows and did odds and ends of repair work around the house and barn. One night, I called my old friend Cody Pfiefer, who was home from Tech, and we met in town for some catching up over a few beers. The other nights I played cards or dominoes with my folks, and once we stayed up late watching an old John Wayne movie, *The Sons of Katy Elder*, one of my favorites.

The fifth day into my break, Dad asked me to check fence lines while he drove to Brownwood to look at a used Bob Cat Skid-Steer Loader somebody had advertised. We had roads along most of the fencing, but the morning was mild and clear and I hadn't ridden since Christmas, so I saddled up Goldie, my favorite dun mare. I tied a 20-gauge behind the saddle in case we happened on a rattler, and I slung a camera around my neck. The camera hobby was one I developed after taking a photography class to fulfill a fine arts requirement at Angelo.

I hit the barbed wire fence line not far north of the house and rode west toward County Road 510. I snapped a couple photos of a tiny patch of early bluebonnets and three or four of a wolf spider hiding at the base of a prickly pear. Not far from where the fence cornered and turned south, I stopped to make a mental note of several small mesquites coming up under the fence. I would come back the next day to spray them. Before I urged Goldie forward again, a late-model Dodge driving south eased to a stop across the fence from me. The man who stepped out wore a pistol on his belt, and I stiffened and reached behind me to lay my hand on the twenty-gauge. He strode to the fence and tipped his Stetson.

"Mornin'," he said.

I nodded. "Something I can help you with?"

He must have noticed that I looked at the pistol on his belt rather than at his face, my right hand behind me on the shotgun. He raised his hands slightly, palms outward. "No harm intended," he said. "I'm a police officer from Argyle. Name's James."

I guided Goldie back his way, stepped down, and walked to the fence. I extended my hand. "I'm Marcus." He nodded and shook my hand. "You're a ways from home," I observed.

"A little. I'm looking for someone."

"Business or pleasure?"

"Neither." He leaned on the top strand of wire, elbows carefully placed between barbs. "Curiosity, mostly."

"About?"

"A man named Needham. Wacy Needham. You know him?"

My stomach tightened. "Yeah, I know him."

"He's my father." He smiled but otherwise exhibited no amusement.

Needham had been married four times before I was even born, but I had heard stories about his four wives, including the second one who bore two children he beat occasionally. He beat the wife, too, until she disappeared with her kids and never contacted him again.

"No offense," I said, "but I don't think you'll like what you find."

"Don't expect to." He straightened, curled the fingers of both hands around the wire between the barbs. He looked past me, not at me. "Just looking for closure, I guess."

I pointed north, the direction he had come from. "His place borders ours. About a quarter mile back. Double gate. Painted black."

He nodded his thanks, then said, "Like his heart."

"Yeah," I said, "black like his heart."

"Much obliged." He tipped his hat.

I didn't have a hat to tip, but as he turned back toward his truck I waved and said, "Good luck."

After he drove away, I mounted Goldie and continued my check of the fence line.

On my way back to the house, I could rouse no interest in taking pictures, distracted as I was by memories of Needham and thoughts about his son James. I tried to imagine what it must have been like for James and his little brother back then, or what it would be like to visit a father who probably didn't give a damn about his son as an adult. I didn't think he'd find much closure in his visit.

That night I dreamed strange dreams of dead dogs and kids with black eyes and bloody lips. In one, Needham lay next to my dog Bo, both of them bleeding from a wound made by a small-caliber rifle.

The next morning, I mixed Remedy and diesel in the sprayer, loaded it into the pickup bed, and drove to the spot I'd seen those young mesquites. I had just finished the spraying when James eased to a stop on the county road.

He got out and walked to the fence corner ahead of me. "Good fences make good neighbors, huh?"

"You know that poem? I read it my sophomore year."

"I don't think Frost believed it," James said. "And it's damn sure not true in your case."

I shrugged. "We do all right. Ignore him mostly."

"You were right," he said. "I didn't like what I found."

"Well," I said, "you tried."

"Know what he told me? Said any beating I got as a kid was well deserved. Told me he wouldn't apologize for anything he'd ever done. Told me if I expected it I should just move on."

I looked at the ground, shook my head. "That's probably best."

He snorted. "Oh, hell yes. Slept in my truck last night."

"Could have stayed here. We have an extra bed."

"Wouldn't impose on strangers."

I nodded. "Well, if anything ever brings you back, consider yourself an acquaintance."

"Appreciate it." We stood quiet for a few seconds, me wondering what to say next. "Listen," he said, "I'm sorry for anything that old bastard did to you or your family."

I shrugged. "Wasn't your fault." I strode to where he stood and extended my hand. We shook.

Sunday morning, Mom fixed a huge breakfast of bacon, fried eggs, grits, and biscuits and gravy. She teared up while I packed my truck, and Dad busied himself with something in the front garden. After goodbyes, I headed back to school, thinking about Needham and what a miserable human being he was. I hate to admit it, but with those thoughts in my head, I was immensely pleased when, nearing Needham's gate on County Road 510, I spotted him hanging upside down from his own fence, one leg tangled between two strands of barbed wire just like a hung deer.

I thought about that deer with the two broken legs. And then I thought seriously about putting Needham out of his misery—and James's and mine.

I eased to a stop and stared for a few minutes, smiling the whole while. Eventually, I stepped out but left my truck running. His pickup sat in front of his gate. He hung from the fence a few feet from there, his face in the dirt. The gate was high and made of vertical steel bars between two cross-bars—virtually unclimbable. He always locked it when he was out. I guessed that, drunk and unable to find his key, he had tried to climb the fence.

He hadn't moved since I'd arrived, and I began to wonder if he was dead, if I had wasted the few seconds I'd spent considering putting him out of his misery.

"You alive?" I hollered. He made no reply. I stepped up to the wire. "Needham, you alive?" He groaned. "Okay," I said. "In that case I'll be on my way."

139

I took about three steps back toward my truck before he said, his voice a gravelly whisper, "Goddamn you!"

I stepped back to the fence. "Looks to me, old man, as if you're the one God damned. You drop your key in the dark again?" I placed my palms between barbs and leaned against the top strand of wire. He grunted. "Damn," I said, "looks like those barbs are gouging pretty good into your calf. You must have struggled pretty hard to wedge them in like that."

He had turned his face so his cheek lay in the dirt. "Cut me out of here, you little shit," he said, his voice still raw.

I clucked my tongue. "That's no way to ask a favor, old man. How about a *please*?"

He grunted and then was silent. After fifteen or twenty seconds, he said hoarsely, quietly, "Please."

"When I was kid," I said, "you killed my dog."

"And you killed mine. I reckon we're even."

I had suspected he knew, but this was my first confirmation. "I wish I hadn't." I gazed back in the direction of my family's property and remembered sobbing after Dad and I buried Bo and then again after I had poisoned his border collie. "But we're not even. I regretted the hell out of what I'd done, and you've never regretted anything in your life."

"I said please."

"You begging?"

"Shit no. Never begged for nothing in my life."

I leaned heavily on the barbed wire. He moaned. "Maybe it's time," I said.

After a few seconds, he said, "Okay, I'm begging." He sounded defeated. I was satisfied. I fetched wire cutters from my tool box, snipped one side of the wires and then the other. He *thunked* to the ground. He lay there for a time, panting and groaning, then finally struggled to his feet.

"I'm sorry," I said, "that I killed your dog."

The blood that had gone to his head during a night upside down drained back out. He wobbled from the draining and maybe from leftover drunkenness. Then he stumbled to his caliche road and walked toward his house.

"You're welcome," I hollered.

I threw the cutters back into the tool box and opened the cab door before I heard him call, "Listen, boy." My hand on the door frame, I turned in his direction. He stood looking small and used up in the middle of his road. He started to speak, then hesitated. He stared at me, then at the ground. He shook his head and slowly looked back at me. "About your dog, I guess maybe I'm sorry I killed him."

We held eye contact for a couple of seconds. Then I offered a half-nod. He didn't return the gesture, just stared. I stepped up into the cab, slammed the door, and dropped the truck into drive. As I eased forward, I raised my left hand out the window and gave him the finger. He stumbled toward his house, his back turned, and didn't see.

Burying Jasper

"You may regret the timing of your visit." Augie Winston yelled to be heard over the thunder, the howling wind, and the slashing rain, the aftermath of a hurricane sent all the way to Bartonville. Local reports warned of tornadoes, a bad time to be outside, but Jasper had to be buried.

Cecil Jubak shook his head. "Nope. Not when my namesake needs all the support he can get."

His namesake, Augie's ten-year-old son, slogged through the mud behind them and sobbed inconsolably. He clutched the drenched body of his best friend to his chest, his Welsh corgi, Jasper.

The boy had sat on the porch, talking to Jasper and stroking his fur while he died. Afterwards, he had pulled the limp body onto his lap and cried. When the rain began, he refused to go inside until Augie wrapped the dog in a large towel and carried it to the laundry room. Young Cecil, still crying, planted himself next to Jasper's body and vowed not to leave his side until he was buried.

Augie, sympathetic with his son's feelings but perturbed by his stubbornness, tried to remain calm. "As soon as the storm is over. But right now, you need to eat." The boy buried his face in the dog's fur and wouldn't budge. "Fine," Augie said, fighting back rising anger at his son's entrenchment. "We'll eat dinner without you."

Augie sat at the table with his wife, daughter, and friend, but he only picked at his baked chicken, mashed potatoes, and peas. When the others finished, he pushed back from the table and said, "Okay." Despite the darkness and the violent storm, he went to fetch shovels.

Now, ten feet from the edge of a small tank—a favorite haunt of young Cecil and Jasper—the boy said between hiccupped sobs, "Here. It's where we were."

Augie turned to him, eased to one knee in the soupy earth, and wrapped his arms around boy and dog.

"Daddy," his son said. "Daddy."

Augie squeezed harder. "I know," he said. He fought the rising lump in his throat. This boy, Cecil William Winston, the son he loved more than his own life, was the boy he had almost deserted when Lily first announced her pregnancy. And Jasper was the puppy he had bought on the day he returned to hugely pregnant Lily. He barely remembered life before that time, couldn't imagine living without Lily and young Cecil and Sybil, his six-year-old daughter.

"It was there," his son said and pointed to a large, jagged, brownish rock next to which the rattler had been coiled. When the boy, cane pole in hand, had stepped past the rock and the warning rattle had sounded, Jasper leapt toward the sound. He misjudged the location just enough to give the snake a chance to strike. The dog had eventually sunk his teeth into his attacker's flesh just behind the head and hadn't stopped grinding until the rattler's head remained connected only by a slender strip of tough skin. By then, though, it had bitten Jasper three times.

"I know to watch," the boy said, his voice cracking into another sob. "I should have been watching."

Augie squeezed him tightly before rising. "It's not your fault," he said and began digging, glad for the drenching rain that disguised his own tears. His friend Cecil joined in the excavation, and no one spoke.

The saturated mud made digging easy, but for every shovelful they removed, rushing water washed half back in. Augie dropped to his knees and with bare hands scooped madly, flinging mud and water far away from the hole. When he paused and leaned back, Cecil immediately dug just as madly, and after four scoops stepped back so Augie could again bail water and loose mud. The boy clung to Jasper and watched the slowly growing hole. At every flash of lightning and crack of thunder, he flinched, but he never took his eyes off the grave.

When he judged that the hole was four feet deep, Augie rose from his soppy perch at its edge. He stepped to his son and held out his hands. The boy pushed his face against Jasper's and then slowly relinquished the dog to his father. Augie leaned over the grave, already filling with water, and gently laid the body in. Cecil plopped the first shovel of nearly liquid mud into the hole before Augie, who had been impatient to get the job done, shoved his hand into the air and shouted, "Wait!" He unclasped a slender silver chain from around his neck and slipped off the small silver heart that dangled there.

Ten years before, shortly after he had returned to Lily, she had given him the necklace. "So you'll know," she had said, "that you'll always have my heart."

Augie shoved the heart into his jeans pocket. He leaned again over the grave and unbuckled Jasper's collar, from which he removed the tag. He threaded the tag onto the chain, which he hooked around his son's neck. "So you'll know," he said. "So he'll always be with you."

The boy nodded solemnly. "But what about Jasper?" he said. "How will he know *we're* with *him*?"

Augie scowled, then peered through the dark and rain at his friend, who looked apologetic and shrugged. Augie's eyes moved to the grave he was eager to fill. "Okay," he said. "How about this?" He unbuttoned his shirt, stripped it off, and laid it over Jasper, now almost submerged in water. The boy stared, then nodded and removed his own shirt. He shivered in the cold rain, and the wind raised goose bumps on his bare skin.

"May I?" Cecil asked. When his namesake nodded again, Cecil followed suit and spread his shirt on top of theirs.

The boy dropped to his hands and knees and leaned close to Jasper's ear. "So you'll know," he whispered.

Augie bailed water from the grave for the last time, and he and Cecil worked quickly to fill the hole. Then the three of them leaned into the wind and rain and trudged, bare-chested, toward home.

IV. Cats and Bluebonnets

Tangled Up in Blue

There is no flash of insight, no moment of clarity, no transcendence. My whole life does not unfold before my eyes.

But as I have heard, and read, and seen in movies, the world does slow down. The storm-whipped oaks and pecans on both sides of the bridge are becalmed, the windshield wipers crawl to a stop, and I can see each individual raindrop explode onto the glass. Then the SUV starts to roll over and over, each deafening impact with the pavement more deliberate than the last. It seems to take a lifetime to flip over the guardrail—my lifetime, what is left of my lifetime—and plunge headfirst into the rain-swollen waters of Hickory Creek. I watch the airbag deploy, feel it scrape my bare thighs and my face, hear glass shatter.

Finally, as cold water begins to pour into the cabin and I cannot seem to find my breath, a flash does come. And clarity. But instead of the bright light of transcendence, I am filled with regret. Then comes the slow unfolding. It is not my whole life opening up before my eyes in slow motion like a Night-Blooming Cereus flower beneath a midsummer's moon; but rather this awful, upside-down, worst of all days. As the dark water closes over me, I see myself standing on the front porch this morning. I hear Augie calling my name.

"Lily!"

In answer, I raised my middle finger in the direction of his white diesel 4X4, a double-cab, with the DOUG PARR CUSTOM HOMES logo splashed in garnet and white along the sides and the stainless steel, cross-bed toolbox that gleamed dully in the early morning rain. I was thinking, not for the first time, that my husband spent more time in that goddamned truck than he did with me.

Augie gunned the engine, spinning the tires on the wet pavement as he tore away from the curb. Driving away from me, and from our never-ending difference of opinion, again. I stepped after him, enveloped in the cloying mix of diesel exhaust and April rain, and misjudged the drop-off from the porch. I stumbled. The high heel broke off my right pump, my ankle twisting painfully. But I refused to go down. With my red-and-white Argyle Eagles umbrella clenched in my left hand and the middle finger of my right still silently screaming hurt and rage at Augie's refusal to hear, I hobbled after him until he fishtailed around the corner and disappeared.

Then I slipped off my high heels, the wet flagstones cool against the soles of my feet as I limped back into the house. The fresh pot of coffee Augie always puts on for me after he fills his thermos had finished brewing, and the house was filled with the scent of fresh-ground French roast. I felt the knot in my belly loosen a little, felt the tightness in my shoulders ease, felt my churning emotions at Augie's refusal to listen settle slowly into a grudging gratitude for the dozen thoughtful things he does for me every day. And I almost picked up my cell phone and called him to apologize for my fit of frustration-born wrath. But I needed to be at the high school early to set up the computer room for end-of-term testing, needed to pick out another pair of shoes, needed to feed the kids breakfast. And I was desperate for coffee. So I poured a cup of French roast into a travel mug, yelled at Cecil and Sybil to get a move-on, and headed for the master bedroom instead.

Fifteen minutes later, we were backing out of the garage. The travel mug—its contents replenished, still lava hot from the microwave—sat in a cup holder, capped for the ride to Argyle High. Cecil and Sybil munched brown-sugar-and-cinnamon Pop-Tarts straight out of the package and slurped Strawberry-Kiwi Capri Suns through straws. I glanced at Sybil in the rearview mirror as I swung the SUV around into the street. She had on pink joggers and a bright orange top, a fashion disaster that I supposed was the inevitable result of an eight-year-old being allowed to pick out her own clothes on a stormy and harried Monday morning. I couldn't make out her shoes. But considering the way the morning was going so far, this was probably a good thing. Cecil, at twelve, had done better: blue jeans, a red Texas Rangers t-shirt, cowboy boots.

"Oh Sybie," I said, trying hard to keep any hint of disapproval out of my voice, "honey, is there by chance a t-shirt back there that you could change into?"

"Are you and Daddy in a fight again?" Sybil asked, the censure that I'd been so careful to keep from my own voice plain to hear in hers.

"They're always in a fight," Cecil said, his tone a ditto of his younger sister's.

"Daddy and I are not always in a fight," I said firmly, looking over my shoulder and making eye contact with Sybil, then with Cecil to my right. "Sometimes we're sleeping," I continued in a husky whisper audible only to myself.

I fixed my eyes onto the rain-slick road, but my mind was on the fighting. The never-ending argument that I'd just half-lied to my children about revolved around another baby: I wanted one, Augie didn't. But the situation was so much more complicated. The baby issue lay at the heart of a tangle of other problems, some larger and some smaller, but all stemming from the fact that we'd been married twelve years, the goals we'd set out to accomplish had mostly been achieved, and for too long a time we'd been occupying the same space with no real connection except the kids. Ever since Augie had been promoted to Construction Manager with Doug Parr Custom Homes—where he supervised and coordinated building for three major housing developments between Fort Worth and Denton—it seemed like all he ever did was work. When he wasn't working, he was exhausted. Despite all the money Augie was making, and the shiny and expensive new things that money was buying for the kids and me, I was unhappy as hell. Our incredible physical connection, the beating heart of our relationship for a decade, had fizzled. The sense of adventure that had driven us to explore new territory and try new things, so in sync with each other's desires that I could draw him across a crowded room just by raising an eyebrow, was gone.

I angled the rearview mirror and raked my eyes across my brand-new black mini-wrap dress, cut so low in front as to be work-wearable only because of the red cardigan I'd buttoned on over it. Underneath the dress were lacy black panties and a sheer black bra. The wrap-around mini emphasized the curves that had come from birthing two children and the lean muscle that had come from working out five days a week for the past year. On top of refusing to listen to a word I had to say this morning, Augie hadn't so much as glanced at the sexy new outfit. But truth be told, I didn't put it on for Augie.

"Stop it, Cecil! Put the radio back on Hot 93.3 where Mom had it!"

Sybil's screech pierced the fog in my head and I glanced down to see Cecil punching buttons on the stereo, flipping from country station to country station—Augie's pre-sets, not mine—to bedevil his sister, whose loathing of country crooners was rivaled only by her hatred of cauliflower. In so many ways, she reminded me of me. Cecil's grin, a carbon copy of his father's, widened as he landed on 92.1: The Possum and started belting out "Okie from Muskogee" in tandem with Merle Haggard. "Leather boots are still in style for manly footwear," Cecil howled in his twelve-year-old falsetto, raising a booted foot so that it was visible to his sister in the back seat. "Beads and Roman sandals won't be seen."

"Stop it! Stop it! Make him stop it, Mom!"

"That's enough!" I switched off the stereo as I swung the SUV into the car line. The shared drop-off (morning)/pick-up (afternoon) lane that looped past both Harpool Middle School and Blanton Elementary was already choked with cars, something I should've anticipated on a stormy Monday: nobody wants their kids to wait on the bus in the rain. "This stops right now."

"Yeah, Cecil."

"That's enough from both of you," I said with a cool resolve I didn't really feel. Then I continued in that same husky whisper from the driveway, audible only to myself, "From all of us."

"Oh Mom," Sybil whined, "you always take his side."

"That's not true. And you know it. But this morning has been especially crazy, and I'd appreciate it if we could all just calm down. Do you think you could do that for your mother who loves you?"

"I will if he will," Sybil said.

"I will if she will," Cecil said.

"Thank you." The car line moved forward in fits and starts, the SUV quiet except for the rain drumming on the roof. And I was just about to pat myself on the back for a solid job of parenting—if not partnering—when it hit me that I'd left the kids' lunches sitting on the counter next to the microwave. When I reached for my purse to dig out lunch money, I realized that I'd left my handbag sitting next to the lunches. "But we've got another problem," I said, after a sickening pause during which I cast about for some option that did not involve my children going hungry or my students showing up to an empty classroom—and found none. "In the rush of getting off this morning, I forgot your lunches. Also, I forgot my purse. I am so sorry."

"No worries, Mom," Cecil said, pat-patting my hand that still rested on the center console where my purse should've been. "I've got a few bucks."

"Me too," Sybil said, the pity in her voice somehow worse than her brother's pat-patting.

"Daddy's got it covered," Cecil said. "He gave us each a twenty to buy snacks at the Rangers game on Saturday, and he let us keep the change."

"I guess that was smart thinking on Daddy's part," I said, stung.

"Daddy's a smart guy," Sybil said.

"Yeah," Cecil said.

"Well," I said, "Mom's smart, too."

The children's silence echoed through the SUV like a slap until we finally reached the drop-off zone. Cecil and Sybil bailed out of the car, their backpacks bouncing as they sprinted through the rain to the front entrances of their respective school buildings without so much as a backward glance. I headed down East Hickory Hill in the direction of Argyle High, trying to get a handle on this whirlwind of a morning, on my relationship with Augie and with the kids—on how I felt about it all. Alienated? Unappreciated? Angry as hell? I stomped the gas pedal, pushing the SUV to the limit on the rain-slick road.

I felt like I needed to see Nick.

Tall, lean-muscled, with a thick salt-and-pepper mustache and piercing gray eyes that seemed always to be focused on me, Nick had hung on every word I said from the moment we met. It was the first day of my long-term substitute teaching job in math at Argyle High School, and I'd come in an hour early to get prepared. Nick sauntered into the classroom that would be mine for two months and introduced himself as "Nick Bynum, the good chemistry guy." He taught in the science lab across the hall, he explained with a sly half-smile, his eyes wandering across me in a lingering glance that ended on my travel mug, filled with the French roast I'd brought from home. "I'm betting you'll need at least one more of those before this first day is through," he said, locking my gaze. "I keep a fresh pot in my classroom all day long. Don't be a stranger."

After a morning spent battling a bunch of teenagers used to torturing substitutes, I basically staggered across the hall when the lunch bell rang. Nick's coffee pot was in the storage room at the back of the lab. We sat at a metal table in the middle of shelf upon shelf of chemicals and lab equipment, and shared sandwiches and cups of strong black coffee. It wasn't long before Nick's much-needed pep talk about handling unruly kids progressed into the two of us exchanging details about each other's lives. When he told me that he'd just moved up to Denton from Jordan in "desert nowhere" Southwest Texas, I asked if he knew May Belle Stiles. The look he gave me was about one-quarter question and three-quarters shocked surprise. "So ... you're into chili?" he sputtered. When I nodded, he blurted, "Best three-alarm in Texas." Then, "And the best damn two-alarm venison chili in the world. Serious chili lovers come to the Second Chance Café on pilgrimages." He leaned across the table and met my eyes. "I'll bet you like it hot." I laughed and said I was a one-alarm kind of girl. Then I told him about the night I'd spent with May Belle and her partner

Arthur Sumps, and how May Belle had been responsible for reconnecting Augie and me.

But the whole time I was talking about Augie, I was thinking about how attracted I was to Nick. It wasn't just that he was in great shape, a swimmer. And it wasn't just that the crow's feet at the corners of his gray eyes perfectly complemented his thick salt-and-pepper hair and his cheesy-cute mustache. In addition to being a great listener, he made me laugh. Every day at lunchtime I'd cross the hall and share Nick's coffee, usually bringing him some baked treat or other from home in exchange—it turned out that he had a sweet tooth—and it wasn't long before I took him into my confidence about the issues between Augie and me. Nick shared details about the women he dated, and gradually things went beyond just flirty. On the Friday before this crazy Monday, we played Twenty Questions, something Augie and I used to do way back when, and the game quickly turned to Nick and me fantasizing about a hook-up. There was no physical contact. Just the fantasy. "What would you do if—?"

The thought of it had haunted me all weekend long.

As I turned onto Hwy 377, five minutes away from Argyle High and Nick, I turned the radio back on. It was still tuned to 92.1: The Possum, and I reflexively moved to switch it back to Hot 93.3, when Lynn Anderson started singing an old Joe South song: "I Never Promised You a Rose Garden." Instead of changing the channel, I cranked it up as loud as it would go. The message in the lyrics—that you have to live right now, just take hold of life and go for what's in front of you, make something out of nothing—was so right on target that it seemed like she was singing it just to me. The hell with sunshine promises, I thought. Embrace the rain. Thinking of Nick, I pulled the lid off the travel mug and savored the steamy-rich scent of the coffee. But when I went to take a sip, I sloshed the lava-hot liquid onto my lap. My thighs felt like they were on fire and I slammed on the brakes, sliding out onto Highway 377 and peeling the hot-coffee-soaked skirt away from my skin. There came a blare of horns and I instinctively stomped on the gas pedal, controlling the skid and accelerating to road speed as I joined the flow of traffic. Then I looked down to see how badly I was burned. The skin on my inner thighs was red, but there were no blisters. And luckily, my dress was black. So the coffee stain wouldn't show.

I swung the SUV into a space in the faculty lot and limped into the building. The pain in my ankle made me glad for the red flats I'd changed into. The lobby outside the principal's office was already packed with kids, and I knew I was running very short on time. So instead of going to my classroom first, I headed straight to the computer lab to get set up for math testing. The kids would be practicing for their end-of-term tests, which would determine whether or not they would move on to the next grade; so even though today would just be a practice run, it was important. At least, I thought as I swung open the door, I'd remembered to bring the key to the computer lab. But as I worked my way around the room, frantically turning on computers as I went, I found an old black refrigerator in the back corner—dented and scratched, and with a lever on the single door instead of a handle—blocking several of the machines. What the hell? After spending precious seconds I didn't have casting through possibilities as to what an antique refrigerator could be doing there, I tried to open it. But the door wouldn't budge. So I set down my bookbag, gripped the lever with both hands, and yanked for all I was worth. The handle came off in my hands, and I stumbled backwards as the fridge door flew open.

Inside, I saw what looked like ... cats.

I inched closer, at the same time repelled and curious, certain that I had to be wrong. But the shelves inside the refrigerator were indeed stacked with cats. Dead cats. Dozens of dead cats of all colors, their limbs spread-eagled and their mouths stuffed with what looked like Styrofoam. And there was a smell. Not rotten exactly, but something that was actually worse—half-chemical and half-decay. I found myself, strangely, feeling relieved that I hadn't eaten any breakfast. Then horror took over, and I slammed the door and ran gagging out of the room.

The science lab was right down the hall and I went there instinctively, trying hard not to throw up. Judging by the look on Nick's face when I barged in, I must've looked like I felt.

"Lily?" he said, wide-eyed. "What—"

"There's a fridge full of dead fucking cats in the computer lab," I groaned. "That's what."

To my complete surprise, I saw Nick grin. He clapped both hands over his mouth, his eyes wide with held-back laughter. Then he went red in the face and it just burst out of him.

"What the hell is so funny about dead cats in the computer lab?"

"It was me," he managed, still laughing out loud. "I was ... I was the one who put the fridge in there. I am so sorry."

"For putting dead cats in the math computer lab, or for laughing at me?"

"For both," he said, wiping his eyes. "But look on the bright side: How could it get any worse?"

"It's worse. When I opened the door, I yanked off the handle."

He burst out laughing again. And this time, I found myself laughing with him. "It isn't funny," I said, still laughing, but on the verge of tears.

"I know, I know. But ... we'll get it fixed. You go ahead. I'll be right there."

I ran back to the computer lab and started trying to fit the lever back onto the refrigerator door. The handle part slid right back on; but when I tried to make the lever work, it fell off the door. It was plain that a piece was missing. Or more likely, pieces. I had just started searching the floor when Nick came in carrying a screwdriver. When I told him what had happened, he immediately knew what the problem was. "You're missing a bolt," he said. "And there should be a nut and a washer to hold it in place." Knowing what I was looking for made my search a little easier. I found the bolt under a computer desk right next to the fridge. The nut and washer had rolled all the way to the other side of the lab, next to the teacher's desk. I handed all three to Nick, and he got busy reattaching the handle.

"Dammit!" Nick said, slamming the screwdriver down onto the desk beside him.

"What now?"

"The screwdriver is too big for the slot in the bolt head. So the nut won't tighten enough for the door to work. We need something thinner."

I rifled through the teacher's desk for something that might work. "There's a pair of scissors in here. How about that?"

I handed the scissors to Nick, and while he was fiddling with the fridge, I sat on the edge of the teacher's desk and fanned myself. I hadn't realized until now how stuffy it was in the computer lab. The machines I'd turned on already had made the atmosphere uncomfortably warm, and the air conditioner didn't seem to be on. Even worse, in addition to the heat and humidity, the smell that had made me gag earlier—half-chemical, half-decay—now filled the entire room.

"My God," I said, slipping off my cardigan and draping it over the back of a chair, "I'm roasting. And that has got to be the worst thing I've ever smelled."

"The cats must've been thawing all weekend," Nick said. "I guess the thunderstorms knocked out the power to the science labs on Friday night, when the front blew in. When I got here this morning, and turned the power back on, the electrical socket wouldn't work. The only other fridge-compatible socket was in the math computer lab. So I hauled it down here. I had no idea that anyone would be in here today."

"So what you're saying is that these moldy dead cats are going to be stored here all day?"

Nick finally managed to get the handle tightened. He opened the door, closed it, opened it again. "It kind of looks that way." He closed the door and stepped back. "But at least the door shuts now."

"Look, after two months of battling teenagers, I know these kids. They are going to open that fridge. Then what? Because the vision that I'm getting of these kids and those dead cats isn't pretty."

"I'll be right back," Nick said. Then he ducked out the door.

In less than a minute, he returned with a roll of gray duct tape. And the two of us taped the refrigerator shut. After six wraps of gray tape at the top of the door, and six gray wraps at the bottom, I was feeling better about the whole thing. And I said so.

"After having spent the better part of a school year battling them, I know these kids myself. They would have opened it for sure. And you're right: the vision isn't pretty."

We started laughing again. Then Nick reached an arm around my waist, sudden and strong, pulled me to him, and kissed me hard. I pulled back at first, involuntarily, then gave myself up to the moment. It seemed unreal, but right somehow, as we groped each other and Nick's kisses found their way to my neck. Next his hands found their way inside my wrap dress, inside my panties and bra, and things were quickly getting beyond just hot and heavy. And even though I knew that the kids could come in at any moment, I didn't care.

Then the first bell rang, and I froze. But Nick kept going.

"Nick," I breathed after an eternal moment, "there's no time."

"You're right," he said, husky-voiced, as he pulled away from me. "Lunch?"

I shook my head. "We're on a testing schedule," I said. "Remember?"

"Whew. You're right. I do remember. After school, then. My place. It's right off 377 in Denton."

"Text me your address. I'll get someone to pick up the kids, and go straight there after the final bell."

With that, Nick headed back to the science lab. I rearranged my dress and buttoned my cardigan back on. And with no time to reserve a back-up computer lab, I had to press on. By the time I'd fired up the rest of the computers, the room was filled with my first class. The kids did indeed want to open the refrigerator—one of them went so far as to try unwrapping the tape—and they all asked about what was inside. I told them it was a biology experiment, and left it at that. The irony of the answer, and the anticipation of Nick's and my own looming biology experiment, kept me smiling throughout the day despite the hassle of the alternate testing schedule—extended periods without interruptions, a shortened lunch—and issues with fridge-obsessed kids. The air conditioner finally kicked on around midmorning, which helped with both the stuffy air and the smell.

Although I didn't get to see him at lunch, I thought about Nick all day. He texted me his address during the second extended testing period. Just the address, nothing else. I replied with: *What will you do when I'm there?* We texted back and forth after that—a replay of our Twenty Questions game from Friday.

But *would* had become *will*.

After Nick's and my Twenty Questions session on Friday, I knew that today was the day we would get together—the day *would* became *will*—if it was ever going to happen. I lingered and flirted with Nick Friday afternoon, and thoughts of our fantasy hook-up filled my mind all through Saturday's rain. But when I lay down next to Augie last night, smelled the familiar and comforting scent of him, I was thinking it was going to be never. This morning though, after our fight and the kids' silence about my intelligence, I was all about now. Now or never, I kept telling myself. This crazy Monday was the last day of my long-term substitute teaching stint at Argyle High. The woman I'd been filling in for was on maternity leave, a fact that Augie had found amusing but that burned me to the core. I kept feeling Nick's hands on my body and tasting his skin. But it was the dead cats that had decided the issue. Truth be told, my affair with Nick was more about being disconnected from Augie than anything else. I felt like Augie had been checked out of our relationship for a long time. On our first date, more than a decade ago, he'd stopped his truck on the side of a country road just to pick me an armload of bluebonnets that he gave me, along with a first kiss, in that field of flowers that seemed to stretch to the end of the world—anyway, to the end of our lifetimes. All that was left of that promise-filled beginning was a fridge full of dead cats and a house full of expensive things bought with the wages of Augie's absence.

I called my mother during the shortened lunch and asked her to pick up Cecil and Sybil. I told her that something had come up, and that I had to stay late after school and sign papers on my last day. The dead cats and bluebonnets I kept to myself. And when the final bell finally rang at 3:40, I texted Nick that I was on my way.

I headed north on 377 toward Denton through heavy rain, my anticipation building with each mile. I had the radio off so that I could hear the GPS directions from my cell phone. And anyway, the drum of the rain on the roof helped keep me from thinking. I'd had enough of thinking—about Augie and me, about the kids, about all of our futures or the lack thereof—to last a lifetime. I never promised you a rose garden, I thought. All I wanted to do today was feel. I tried to keep my eyes on the road, and my mind on the promise of physical pleasure. Today, I would embrace the rain.

But there was road construction on Highway 377. They were working on an overpass, and dump trucks and heavy equipment lined both sides of the roadwork-narrowed lanes. As I cleared the construction zone, I glanced to my right and caught sight of a field of blue in the rain. Bluebonnets, I realized, royal blue and beautiful, stretching away under the lead-gray sky. Despite my resolve to focus only on feeling, I suddenly found myself thinking about promises instead—about all that went with them, about what they sometimes meant we had to do without—and I realized, with a pain that was as physical and real as a spear through my chest, that I was making a terrible mistake. I still loved Augie, and I always would.

And seeing nothing but Augie with his arms brimful of bluebonnets on a clear April day, I slammed on the brakes. I felt the SUV start to slide sideways toward another patch of road construction, guardrail work on the Hickory Creek Bridge. The world started to slow, then to spin, then to flip over and over, blue then gray, blue/gray, black.

2.

The way Ralph saw it, Uncle Billy Rey picked an inconvenient time to need burying, but speaking such an idea, Ralph told himself, could get him in a heap of trouble. His brother and sister, if they came to the funeral, would surely accuse him of being the same as he ever was, and their view of him, Ralph knew, wasn't good. Not good at all, though he thought it best not to tell Lily how his siblings viewed him.

Lily sat in a chair in her tiny hospital room, wearing a hospital gown, a skimpy one that Ralph liked. He glanced at her to take in as much of her pretty body as he could without her catching him. She seemed unaware of such glances. "Did you know your uncle well?" she asked.

"Barely knew him at all, but he is family, so I need to go."

"Of course."

"I'll be back around noon, about the time the doctors release you. I should have you home by two or earlier."

"You're doing so much for me. Too much. But I appreciate you more than I can say."

Ralph nodded, understanding her gratitude, liking it. He had, after all, saved her from drowning. Or his brother had saved her, he corrected himself. But he did help, he knew, enough to enjoy her gratitude.

When Lily had regained consciousness and the docs allowed Ralph to see her, she listened with great intensity to how Ralph and James pulled her from the car, revived her, and took her to the hospital. When he finished the account, Lily astounded him by talking about what led her to the accident, her troubled decision to start an affair with a colleague, and how, at the last minute as the car flipped into the water, she knew in a flash that the decision to have sex with Nick was a bad one.

Ralph felt pleased that she confided in him, that she trusted him, and trust was something he knew he had seldom earned. Lily's trust, he thought, just might be worth all the crappy therapy he had to endure recently.

At the funeral, people Ralph didn't know stood around in little groups, some moving in and out of the open-air chapel in the cemetery. Others still in their cars nosed around the winding cemetery roads, pausing, Ralph figured, to ask which of the three burial groups was the one for Billy Rey Thomson. A guy wearing a baseball cap, a t-shirt that maybe was once red, and jeans ripped on both knees wandered close to Ralph and spoke in a loud whisper: "Do you know the name of that lady over there? The one in red."

Ralph considered the woman. "No. The only one I know here is Billy Rey." He started to add, "you know, the one in the urn," thought better of it, and asked himself why he was whispering.

Ball cap man nodded. "Who are all these people, anyway?" the man wandered into the chapel.

Another loud whisper came from behind Ralph: "You doing okay today?"

"Okay enough."

"Did she talk after I left?"

Ralph knew if he turned he would see his brother. "She talked a great deal," Ralph said. "And why is everybody whispering?" He let a note of annoyance creep into his voice.

"Did you get her name?"

"Yes." When Ralph turned around, he fought back his irritation over seeing his brother in full police regalia. "Hello, James."

"So what is her name?"

"Lily."

"When did she regain consciousness?"

Ralph raised his voice above a whisper. "Not long after she got to the hospital yesterday. The docs say she can check out this afternoon."

"Did she remember the accident?"

"Only that her car flipped and landed in the water. No memory at all of our pulling her out. It was news to her that you saved her with CPR."

"What is her last name?"

Ralph crossed his arms and stepped back. "She didn't want to say."

James waved at someone parking a car. "Our sister is here."

"Do you stay in touch with our sister?"

"Some. Look, Ralph, I need to know Lily's last name to complete my report to the Argyle police."

"Maybe she'll be ready to give you that information this afternoon."

"So you're going back to see her again? What on earth for?"

Ralph shook his head in frustration. "Why would you ask that? We saved her life, and we owe her for our involvement. We owe her."

"Owe her what?"

"Follow-through. Something I've been short on for most of my life, as you and Laverne and Mom have always been so fast to point out. Follow-through." Ralph could tell from his brother's perplexed look that he had no idea what *follow-through* meant, and that's damned irritating, he thought. But surely Laverne would know.

"I guess it doesn't matter much if she doesn't want to give her last name. The towing boys will drag that car out of the creek today, and the police will have access to her credentials in her purse and to her license plate. I'll have her name today."

"It's a personal matter about her and her husband," Ralph said. "She doesn't want him to know yet what she was doing driving so far, and in the rain."

"An affair, then," James said.

"Not quite, but close." Ralph felt some surprise that his brother had hit so near to home in his guess about Lily. But then, Ralph thought, he is a cop. A *cop*, he told himself again, trying not to dislike the word, trying to recapture the new attitude about the law that he thought he learned in counseling sessions.

As a condition of their mother's will, Ralph had gone to all the counseling recommended by Dr. Brubaker at the Amarillo Pavilion, including several bouts of group therapy and something the doc called sensitivity training. It seemed likely to Ralph that his sister Laverne had pushed the doc to list as many kinds of counseling as possible. The interfering witch, he thought, then warned himself against that sort of negative thinking. He admitted to himself, again, that his alcohol and drug abuse had gotten a bit out of hand.

When she joined him and James, Laverne spoke little and was soon walking from group to group of the mourners, though Ralph saw no one doing any mourning or even looking particularly sad, something he mentioned to James.

"But of course," James said. "Uncle Billy Rey drank too much, and he did that every day for the last few years. When drunk he was always verbally abusive to anyone in earshot. I doubt anyone here liked him, not even his son. Maybe years ago they did, but he changed minds fast with his cantankerous and alcoholic ways. That woman over there in black with the red bow? She was Billy Rey's partner for years, left him some time back. It's a surprise to see her here. In a way it is a bit of a surprise to see anyone here. I didn't much like the old curmudgeon, either."

Laverne joined them in the open-air chapel where Billy Rey's son gave a brief statement about his father and made a few languid motions toward the urn and the photo beside it. No one shed tears, Ralph noticed.

At the end of what passed for a service, everyone left except for some immediate family members: two of Billy Rey's brothers and their wives, a grandson—the one wearing a baseball cap—and Ralph, standing in awkward silence beside James and Laverne.

At first Ralph was puzzled about the nature of the discussion among the family. There was some sort of disagreement and people raised their voices. It became clear that they were discussing what to do with Billy

Rey's ashes. One brother said, "We could scatter him around the cemetery." The others nodded, and the brother picked up the urn.

"This is not good," James whispered, then stepped forward. "It's illegal to scatter human ashes in the cemetery."

Baseball cap man spoke up, his tone proclaiming he had a good solution: "We could dump him over that fence there at the edge of the cemetery." Several people nodded.

Laverne moved closer to the group. "Now wait," she said. "Because you can't scatter Billy Rey's ashes in the cemetery, you want to throw them into someone else's yard for them to have to deal with the problem?" She delivered the message in an accusatory tone that Ralph knew all too well from his dealings with his sister. The relatives looked at the ground, none seeming able to meet her gaze but all wearing a stubborn, unyielding look on their faces.

It went against Ralph's nature to join such a discussion, but he drew upon some of his new empathy, learned in one of his group counseling sessions in Amarillo. "Billy Rey loved fishing in Hickory Creek. Why not scatter his ashes in the creek water?"

Laverne looked at him in surprise. "What a wonderful suggestion," she said.

"But that's a good twenty miles away," one brother said, and several others agreed.

"I went fishing a bunch of times in that creek with Uncle Billy Rey," Ralph said. "I would be pleased to scatter him in Hickory Creek."

James and Laverne stared, a response that pleased Ralph, though he also felt a bit surprised by his offer.

The relatives glanced at each other, most of them nodding, and baseball cap man picked up the urn, handed it to Ralph.

"I have a call to make. Hold this." Ralph handed the urn to Laverne. He took out his cell phone and stepped outside the small chapel.

Lily answered right away. "They're ready to check me out. Are you sure you're okay about driving me home?"

"I'll be there within an hour," Ralph said. He told her about the funeral, about his offer to scatter his uncle's ashes, about his sister holding the urn.

"Take me with you to Hickory Creek Bridge," Lily said. "I want to see where I nearly drowned. You are a good man, Ralph McKneely, and I would like to meet your sister and brother. I would like to take part in the ceremony of scattering ashes, if you are okay with that."

Back with James and Laverne, Ralph thought it best to tell them about Lily's request, but before he could get a word out, Laverne said, "You never liked fishing."

"You never spent any time at all with Uncle Billy Rey," James said.

"For sure you never went fishing with him," Laverne said.

"So?" Ralph asked.

"So you're doing something remarkable for a family that's full of anger," James said. "But—"

"But," Laverne interrupted, "your good act is based on lies."

Ralph took the urn from Laverne. "Didn't Mom tell us that a lie that accomplishes something good can be worthy of being called a truth?"

"Yes," Laverne said. "Your lie led to your offer of a good deed, so the lie is positive in an odd sort of way, and I suppose it equals truth, at least in Mom's way of thinking. But sitting firmly on your lie, the deed is tainted."

That tone, again, Ralph thought, the accusatory one, the condemning one he had heard so many times from his sister, is wrong and unfair and worse than his paltry little fib.

"Maybe," James said, "we can lessen the taint by helping scatter the ashes. Neither of us has told lies about fishing or creeks."

"Has the whole damn world gone nuts?" Ralph demanded.

"James is right," Laverne said. "When do we do it? Right now?"

"First I need to tell you about taking Lily home."

"Is this Lily a girlfriend?" Laverne demanded.

"Ease up," James said. "Lily is not his girlfriend. She is a woman Ralph saved from drowning."

Ralph eyed his brother with suspicion, wondering why James chose to lie about the matter, for in Ralph's view, it was James who saved Lily.

James had set up the lunch meeting with Ralph, which brought the two of them to the right spot at the right time for pulling Lily from the water.

It was James who had told his brother about the road construction company near Argyle, about their needing workers. So Ralph, fresh from too damn many Amarillo counseling sessions to suit him, drove to Denton, interviewed for a job, and was hired to help with repairs to Highway 377. In the past, Ralph would have spurned such hard physical labor if he happened to have enough money in his pocket for his next meal and his next bottle. But he believed he should take a job even though he had a bundle of money. His completion of the counseling meant his sister had given him cash due to him from their mother's will. He loosely resolved to save the windfall for doing something good, for a change. So he felt he ought to take the job James had found for him.

The day of the accident James suggested that they meet for lunch by the Hickory Creek Bridge, near where Ralph's job had taken him. James brought burgers from the Argyle Dairy Queen, and the brothers sat in James's patrol car to eat because of the sudden downpour.

When a car flipped in such a dramatic way and plunged into the water, James dropped his burger, jumped from his vehicle, and threw himself into the creek.

Ralph followed, wondering if he should take off his heavy boots, a fleeting thought as he dove in. He found James underwater struggling with the door. Ralph pulled him aside and used his steel-toed boots to kick out the window and his Kabar lock-back to slice through the seatbelt that gripped the woman. Then Ralph headed to the surface for air.

"James pulled Lily from the submerged car," Ralph told Laverne. "He swam her ashore, he administered CPR. James saved her. Hell, I don't even know CPR."

With a dismissive sweep of his hand, James said, "We took her to the hospital in Denton, I driving with the siren and lights on, Ralph following in his car. The emergency crew told me that she would likely be okay, but they needed to make sure she suffered no brain damage."

"I put on dry clothes from my car," Ralph said, "then went back into the hospital, and James returned to Argyle to his cop job. They moved Lily to a private room where she talked to me. A lot of talk, and I ended up telling her I would drive her home."

"You did?" Laverne asked. "Why?"

"We saved her life," Ralph said. "I thought it best to do some follow-through."

Laverne nodded. "I think I'd like to meet her."

"Doesn't Lily have a family?" James asked. "Why are you driving her home?"

"Long story," Ralph said. "She didn't want to tell her husband where she was going when she hit that bridge, so she gave the hospital folk only her first name and no other information."

"Wait," James said. "Her purse has got to be back in that submerged car. How is she paying the hospital when she leaves?"

"I paid. She said she would pay me back, but I don't care if she does or doesn't."

165

"Wow," Laverne said.

"Yeah," James said. "Wow."

"So you are already giving away your inheritance?" Laverne slit her eyes in making her question into an accusation.

"And I always thought you approved of good will and generosity."

"I do, but there needs to be some sensible limits. You don't even know that woman."

"Our brother," James said, "has done some remarkable and unselfish things, and I think he deserves some credit."

"Thanks for that, at least," Ralph said. "I know a great deal about Lily, who doesn't deserve your tone. Her name is Lily, not *that woman*. I just now told her on the phone about scattering Uncle Billy Rey's ashes in Hickory Creek, and you know what *that woman* said? She said she would like to help with the ceremony."

"Ralphie, you keep surprising me. Now I for sure want to meet the woman."

"Lily," Ralph said.

"Well okay, then," Laverne said. "Lily."

"And I haven't been *Ralphie* for years. Years."

"Maybe," Laverne said.

On their way to the Denton hospital in James's police car, Ralph considered telling his siblings about Lily's decision to meet her co-worker, Nick, about how attractive Lily had found him, about how troubled she became over her decision, about her regret, about the car crash coming as she decided to stay with her husband.

But, Ralph asked himself, why should I betray Lily's confidence? And even as he asked, he knew the answer: because he wanted Laverne's approval for the advice he had given Lily. He was certain he understood Nick, knew Nick to be a dishonest predator much as Ralph himself had been before he promised himself he would reform.

From what Lily told him of the progress of her intimacy with Nick, Ralph figured Nick saw Lily's distress in her marriage, offered sympathy and a hug at precisely the right time, and waited. Her trip that took her to the Hickory Creek Bridge would have been his sexual pay-off for his careful timing and patience, had it not been for the accident.

"Stay away from Nick," Ralph had told Lily. "Go back to your family. Never again allow Nick to offer sympathy, never be alone with him. He is simply out for a conquest."

Lily had nodded, her eyes brimming with tears.

Ralph knew he was right because he would have behaved the same way as Nick with such an attractive and troubled woman. Or he would have before he worked at reforming, at becoming a better person.

Telling Laverne about his advice to Lily would, Ralph realized, be a confession that he himself had honed some despicable skills in seducing women, that his "wise" counsel wasn't based on wisdom so much as on his being, essentially, a bad man.

Sitting in the back seat of the patrol car with his siblings in the front, James driving, Ralph slapped his leg, and said, "Damn."

Laverne turned to him. "What is that about?" she demanded.

3.

Augie Winston sat at a corner table in a Hilton Garden Inn. From there he could see the front doors and lobby, and as he sipped his Maker's Mark on the rocks he watched weary travelers drag their wheeled baggage toward the desk for late check-in. A few couples left for or returned from a night out.

"Last call, sweetie," he heard a female voice from across the room. She was the lone waitress left, he the lone customer. He held his glass at eye level, checked the depth, swigged the remainder, then held the empty at arm's length in the waitress's direction. She nodded. Although no alert had sounded, he checked his cell.

"There you go, hon." The waitress set a small napkin in front of him and centered the drink on the napkin. Augie looked up from his phone, attempted a smile, and nodded. He looked back at his phone, then set it face-down on the table and sipped the new drink. "Listen," the waitress said, "none of my business, but are you okay?"

Augie looked back up with that same half-smile. She appeared roughly his age. He noticed a few hints of developing wrinkles, but her eyes were vibrant blue, which made her look younger than she probably was. Her smile revealed neat rows of obviously whitened teeth. She was pretty in a plain way, he thought, and lowered his eyes to take in the rest of her body.

"You have kids?" he asked.

She nodded and sighed. "Three. Fourteen, twelve, and nine. They're a handful. You?"

"Boy and a girl. They can be a handful, too."

"You miss them, huh? I mean, when you're traveling like this."

"Yeah," Augie said and didn't bother mentioning that he lived in Argyle, that he and his wife had argued that morning—as they did every morning these days—or that despite his calls and texts to her, she hadn't replied all day. His eyes wandered over the waitress again, the same way that morning they'd wandered over Lily's sexy black dress—short, tight, with a plunging neckline that revealed plenty of beautiful cleavage. But her nagging hadn't been conducive to romance, and his only thought was to wonder why she'd wear that dress to work. Most likely for that guy—Nick— she had spoken of so often and so fondly, contrasting his attentiveness with Augie's lack thereof.

He looked back into the waitress's blue eyes. "So you're getting off soon, huh?"

"When you're finished." She laid her palm lightly on his shoulder. "But don't hurry on my account. My sister has the kids all night and I'm a single mom. I got nowhere to be." She turned to leave but he put his hand on her forearm to stop her. "Something else?" she asked.

He released her arm and glanced over at his phone. He looked back, held eye contact with her for a few seconds, and finally shook his head. "I guess not."

Augie watched a young couple enter through the sliding doors and stagger toward the elevator. Despite unsteadiness, the woman walked briskly ahead, clicking her high heels loudly against the tile floor. The man walked more sluggishly, scuffing his boot heels, shoulders slumped. At the elevator doors, they looked briefly at each other and then away. He said something to her, but she crossed her arms over her chest and didn't respond. She stared up at the lighted number above the elevator door, shifted her weight to the right, then to the left.

Augie shuddered. He drained his drink, ice clinking against the bottom of the glass when he lowered it from his lips. He rose and carried it to the bar. The waitress smiled, dumped the ice into the sink, and began to wash the glass. "If you're not finished, I could manage a couple more off the record." She ran water into the glass, swirled it to rinse the soap off the sides. A few strands of her auburn hair fell across her face.

"A couple?" Augie said.

She shrugged. "I'm going off the clock. I might have one." She set the glass upside down on a towel, stepped back in front of Augie, and pressed her palms against the counter. "So?"

He reached out, touched her cheek with his fingertips. "I'd love to, but—"

She waved her hand to dismiss the rest of his sentence. "I get it. I'm sorry."

"No, don't be sorry." He leaned across the bar and kissed her cheek. "I'm the one who's sorry."

She turned slightly and brushed her lips across his. "It's okay."

Brief as it was, he felt the softness and warmth of her lips, something he hadn't felt from Lily in a very long time. "About those drinks, could we take them to my room?"

"Yes," she said. "We could."

She flipped two clean, dry glasses over, scooped a little ice into each, and slid the Maker's from the shelf.

Augie watched. "I should tell you," he said, "I'm a little broken right now."

She handed him one of the drinks and smiled halfheartedly. "Aren't we all?" She tapped the rim of her glass against his. In the morning, she rolled out of bed before him. He watched her bend over the sink, wearing panties and his t-shirt, and wash her face. "I'm sorry," he said.

She finished drying her face, hung the towel up, and looked at him in the mirror. "No need."

"It's embarrassing."

She shrugged. "It happens." She uncapped the complimentary mouthwash, drained it, rinsed, gargled, and spit into the sink. "Anyway, I enjoyed sleeping with a warm man. It's been a while." She padded to the bedside, sat on the edge, laid her hand on his chest. "The rest doesn't matter so much."

Augie lifted her hand to his lips, kissed it, then kept his grip on it. "You're a good woman."

She stared intently into his eyes. "What about your wife?"

"My wife?"

She pulled his hand up in front of his face, pointed at the plain gold wedding band encircling his ring finger. "Your wife."

"Yeah, she's a good woman, too. Or used to be."

"Do yourself and her a favor. Either make things right or divorce her." She leaned in and kissed him lightly on the lips. Then she rose, gathered her clothes from the floor, and dressed. Augie watched. "Gotta run, sneak out the back door before anyone knows I was here all night." As she rounded the corner to the door, she looked back briefly and blew him another kiss. He closed his eyes. The door clicked shut.

Later, he called in sick and ordered a large breakfast from room service. He ate in bed and then found an old John Wayne western on television. He tried to concentrate on it, but his thoughts wandered to Lily, and he thought about the waitress's advice: *make things right or divorce her.*

He had tried to make things right, to explain it to her. But she refused to listen. *You're married to your work,* she'd bitch. *Me, the kids, we don't even know you anymore.* Damn, why couldn't she understand that everything he'd ever done was for her and the kids, to give them the best life they could have, the kind of life he never knew in younger days? But she didn't understand, and he didn't know how to make it right. Divorce her? Never. He would never desert Lily and the children the way his parents deserted him.

Make it right! He winced at the sound of the voice next to his bed. But not the waitress's voice. Instead, a voice he'd heard before, the same voice that had spoken to him years ago when Lily announced her first pregnancy and he bolted. It was a demanding voice back then and it was just as demanding now: *Make it right.*

Halfway through the movie, he rolled out of bed, showered, dressed, and checked out.

A block from his house, he spotted a car backing out of his driveway. He looked closely as it passed him leaving the neighborhood. A man, about his age. Heat rose to Augie's face, and anger crept into his chest. That son of a bitch—Nick. Augie had never met him, but he felt sure he was the man driving that car. He had wondered before whether Lily had, in heart and possibly in body, already left the marriage. Maybe that little black dress sealed the deal. He cranked his truck's wheel hard left, hit the opposite curb, slammed the gear shift into reverse, then back into drive, and spun his tires when he punched the gas hard. A block and a half later, he rode the bumper of the other car, emergency flashers blinking and horn blaring. The car slowed and eased to the side. Augie pulled up beside it, stomped his brakes, shoved the shift into park, and flung open his door, the engine still running.

"Get out," he yelled at the man as he rounded his truck and stormed toward the other driver's door. "Get the hell out now!"

The man unbuckled and opened his door. Augie reached over the door, clutched his shirt collar, and dragged him. By the hand full of collar, he pulled the man around the front of the car and to the curb, then raised a fist and swung at his face. The man stumbled back, tripped on the curb, and went down hard on his back.

"Shit," Augie said and flapped his hand, feeling the pain where a tooth had caught one knuckle.

"Shit," the man on the ground said. He cupped his hands over his nose and mouth. "You broke my damn nose!"

Augie sucked blood from his knuckle and spat on the knee of the stranger's jeans. "That's not all I'll break, you son of a bitch." He stepped up the curb, cocked his knee, and raised his booted foot, aiming the toe at the man's ribs. "You'll wish you'd never screwed my wife."

The man shoved bloody hands, palms out, toward Augie. "Wait. I'm not the guy. I saved Lily's life."

Augie dropped his foot to the ground. "Her life? What happened? Is she okay?"

"Yes. Some cuts and bruises, but she's okay."

"The kids. What about the kids?"

"Not in the accident. With her mother."

Augie offered a hand to help him up. The man clutched it and grunted as he hauled himself up. Blood splattered his cheeks and ran from his nose and lips. "Talk fast," Augie said.

"My name's Ralph. Lily flipped her car at Hickory Creek Bridge. Where the construction is. Ended upside down in the water. My brother and I, we saved her." Ralph paused, gently laid a finger against his bloody broken nose, winced. "I just brought her home from the hospital and am on my way to pick up prescribed pain killers."

Augie grabbed for his wallet, slid out three hundreds, and shoved them toward Ralph. "Go get the meds. And stop at a clinic to have that nose checked."

Ralph shook his head. "No need for that." He nodded at the bills in Augie's outstretched hand.

Augie dropped the bills and they fluttered to the ground. "Take them." He spun, trotted to his truck, cranked it around, and sped toward his house.

When Ralph returned, nose bandaged, two hours later, Augie sat on the edge of the bed holding Lily's hand while she slept. Ralph quietly laid a pharmacy bag on the bedside table and backed out the door. Augie released Lily's hand and followed. He pushed the bedroom door almost closed and nodded down the hall toward the living room. When they got there, Augie turned toward the kitchen. "Need a beer?"

"No," Ralph said, then, "Well, yeah, I guess so." He trailed Augie to the refrigerator. "I quit drinking a while back, but I could damn sure use something right now."

Augie handed him a Shiner and took one for himself. They sat at the kitchen bar. "She's been sleeping. I haven't talked to her."

"It was bad," Ralph said. "But she's okay. Doctor said pain medication and lots of rest." He sounded as if he had a cold, and Augie noticed a wad of gauze peeking out of one nostril.

"I'm sorry. You know, about your nose."

"It's not the first time."

"I shouldn't have. Not without knowing."

Ralph shrugged. "It happened. It's over."

Augie nodded. "So, about Lily, what the hell happened?"

Ralph hesitated as if carefully considering his answer. "She flipped over the guardrail. Car landed upside down in the creek." He hesitated again, shook his head. "Thank God my brother and I saw it. We went in after her."

"What the hell was she doing out there?"

Ralph shrugged and avoided eye contact.

Augie frowned. "When I hit you, you said, *I'm not the guy.* So who is?"

Ralph took a swig of his Shiner. "Look, I was just trying not to get hit again."

"So you *are* the guy?"

"No. No. God no. But I wasn't thinking about my specific language."

"But you know."

"No." Ralph took another swig, then another. He looked up at the ceiling. He sighed. "Okay, I don't know who the guy is, but I do know that she had the wreck because she changed her mind. She got distracted, you know, when she decided she couldn't go through with it, slammed on the brakes, and slid out of control."

Augie slid his forefinger down the neck of his bottle, drawing a line in the condensation there. "I know who it is. A guy she works with and talks a lot about." He gripped the bottle tightly, as if trying to shatter it with his hand. "I'm going to kill him."

Ralph leaned back in his chair, stared hard at Augie, shook his head. "Not worth it. You'd go to jail. He's a piece of shit, but not worth it."

"He wanted to screw my wife."

"But she changed her mind. That's what's important. She thought of you and couldn't do it."

The two made eye contact, and Augie smiled an unhappy smile. "He *is* a piece of shit."

"But not worth it." Ralph leaned forward, elbows on the table. "Look, I don't know you, and I don't really know Lily. But she told me some things. She loves you, man. She needs you."

Augie felt the heat in his eyes, and to avert the tears, drained his bottle. He set it down and stared at the table top. "Yeah, I need her, too." He stood up suddenly. "Another one?" Ralph held up his bottle, still mostly full, and shook his head. Augie grabbed another for himself. "So, Ralph, I'm sure you've got things to do, but could you stay a while?"

"You going to kick his ass?"

"That's the plan."

"Then I'll stay."

"Thanks, I won't be too long." Augie returned the unopened beer to the refrigerator.

"Just don't kill the piece of shit," Ralph said.

Headed toward the door, Augie looked back over his shoulder. "I won't, but he may wish I had."

Ralph raised his beer in an approving salute.

Although Augie spotted no active construction work, redirected traffic clogged the highway near Hickory Creek Bridge and slowed his progress. Near the bridge itself, he spotted the twisted guard rail bulging outward toward the creek. He guessed that Lily's car had rolled, hit the rail, and flipped right over. He slowed even more and eased off onto a pad made for parking heavy machinery. He stopped next to a bulldozer. He stared ahead at the grotesquely twisted rail, and his eyes burned again. It was his fault, her accident. She was right, he knew, had known all along but had been too stubborn to admit it. Determined as he'd been to give his family a better life than he had known, he'd lost himself in his work and lost that very family in the process. He stepped out onto the caliche, slick from rain the day before, and sloshed across it to the narrow, paved shoulder, then turned and made his way to the spot where Lily must have gone over. He scanned the creek below, thought of Lily, of the way she must have panicked in the water, immersed and upside down with no escape. Or, maybe she had been unconscious, oblivious to her impending death. He bent slightly, his chest tight, his eyes searing. The creek flowed smoothly, calm and brilliant in the afternoon sun. When he straightened and looked up, away and across from the creek, he saw a carpet of blue through blurry eyes. Bluebonnets, he thought, and he knew what he had to do. Nick could wait; Augie could deal with him later if necessary.

Back at the house, his clothes wet from crossing Hickory Creek, Augie found Ralph still at the kitchen table, playing solitaire, his still nearly full beer pushed off to the side. Ralph looked up from the cards. "Did you do it?

Augie shook his head. "How is she?"

"Checked on her twice. The second time she opened her eyes. I gave her the meds. She asked about you. I told her you were here, worried, and would talk to her when she felt up to it. Then she was out."

Augie retrieved the beer he hadn't opened earlier, twisted the cap, took a swig. "Listen, Ralph, I owe you. You're out a lot of time and probably money. Just tell me, what do I owe you?"

"Nothing." Ralph shook his head. "I haven't been a good person, but lately I've been trying to make it right. This—" he rolled his head to indicate their situation—"this has helped. That's enough." He rose, shook Augie's hand, and headed for the front door.

"You've made it right," Augie called after him. "And now I want to do the same. Just tell me what I owe."

His hand on the door knob, Ralph looked back. "Okay," he said, "this is what you owe me: Do the same. Make it right."

Augie smiled and nodded, but Ralph was already out the door.

Augie set his beer on the table and walked to the bedroom. Lily lay on her back, eyes open, staring at the ceiling. "Lily," he said.

Her head shifted on the pillow. "Augie."

He clutched her hand. "Lily, I'm sorry."

Her hand remained limp. "No, please don't. I tried to cheat on you."

"But you didn't." He squeezed her hand harder. And without a plan and without thinking, he said, "I tried to cheat on you, too."

Lily's eyes opened wider. "With who?"

He shrugged. "This woman at a bar. She came to my room."

"Jesus." She slurred the name. "A drunk bar slut?"

"No, it wasn't like that." Augie's head swam. Why had he said anything? "She was sober. She was a waitress."

"But you climbed into bed with her."

"But I couldn't do it," he said. "Like you. I couldn't."

"Jesus, Augie."

He hung his head, ashamed by what he knew she was thinking. She had damn near died because she'd changed her mind. He, on the other hand, had really tried, had taken a woman whose name he didn't even know to bed, had tried but failed. He felt beyond shamed. He felt dirty. Then he remembered the bluebonnets. "Don't move," he said unnecessarily. "Don't go anywhere. I'll be right back."

He ran down the hall and to the garage, where he scooped the flowers off his back seat. Back in the room, he eased onto the edge of the bed and shoved the bouquet in front of her. "For you," he said.

Her eyes, closed when he sat, fluttered open, just slits until she saw what he held. She smiled weakly. "Bluebonnets." She reached one hand out to clutch them and pulled them to her chest. "Bluebonnets." Her eyes drifted closed again.

"Please, Lily," Augie said.

"So tired," she slurred. "The drugs. So tired." And then she was silent, breathing softly, slowly.